No Safe Harbors

No Safe Harbors

Stephanie S. Tolan

. . .

Charles Scribner's Sons · New York

Copyright © 1981 Stephanie S. Tolan

Library of Congress Cataloging in Publication Data
Tolan, Stephanie S.   No safe harbors.
Summary: At sixteen, Amanda Sterling cannot
accept all the values her parents' lives
represent, but neither does she want to believe
that her father can be guilty of taking a bribe.
I. Title.
PZ7.T5735No   [Fic]   81–14475
ISBN 0–684–17169–4   AACR2

1 3 5 7 9 11 13 15 17 19   F/C   20 18 16 14 12 10 8 6 4 2

Printed in the United States of America

For Robert
who has given me the river,
the harbor,
and sometimes the storm

No Safe Harbors

·1·

Amanda Sterling leaned against the arch that connected the kitchen with the wide front hall. It was 7:30 A.M. of the tenth rainy June day in a row, and her long legs, beneath the extra-large T-shirt she slept in, were still winter-white. "If it goes on like this, there will be mushrooms growing out of the couch!" she said.

James Sterling looked over the top of the newspaper he was reading. "What are *you* doing up?"

Amanda rubbed her eyes and joined her father at the kitchen table. "I've had enough sleep since school let out to last all summer. Soaps and sleep. What else is there to do in this weather?"

Peg Sterling, in white jeans and a hand-embroidered work shirt covered by a clean apron, turned from the scrambled eggs she was tending on the stove. "Steve had some ideas yesterday. You didn't exactly jump at any of them."

Amanda slipped down in her chair, stretching her legs under the table, and picked up her father's coffee cup. He grinned and slapped at her hand. She took a sip before putting the cup back in its saucer and sighed elaborately. "Stephen's ideas have centered around the pinball game in his rec room for months!"

"If I remember correctly, he suggested tennis at the club and a movie yesterday."

1

Amanda made a face. "The only movie we haven't seen in this hick town . . ."

"Hold it!" her father said.

"Okay. Strike the 'hick town.' The only movie we haven't seen yet is that one about the axe murderer. And the indoor courts are full of housewives escaping the kiddies."

"It seems to me," Peg Sterling said, dishing eggs onto two plates, "that you and Steve ought to be able to find something worth doing, rain or no rain. Even without the boats, life does go on."

"I know. I know. That's what I learn from the soaps. Anyway, I didn't feel like spending the day with Stephen yesterday."

James Sterling folded the paper and set it on the table as his wife put his plate on the quilted place mat in front of him. He took his napkin out of its ring and smoothed it across his knees. "Problems?" he asked.

Amanda smiled at him. "No problems, Dad. I guess I'm just bored. It's all this rain! I think I'm rusting solid—like the tinman. It isn't exactly a normal summer."

Peg Sterling sat down at her place. "School's only been out for two weeks. How you can be this bored already I don't understand. Besides, staying home alone all day can't do anything for boredom. At least you could get out with the other kids."

"You mean Steve."

"Not just Steve. You aren't seeing anybody. What's Julie doing? Or Kit?"

Amanda shrugged. "Julie's working at that day camp. Kit's mostly been at the club—with Mark. You don't want me to come between them, do you?"

Her mother's green eyes flashed. "All right, Amanda. Have it your way. Stay here and be bored. But there are

2

things you could do, you know. They need volunteers at the hospital. Maybe this rain's telling you something. Maybe this is the summer to do something for someone else instead of spending all your time on the river. Haven't you any social conscience at all?"

Amanda glanced at her father, who immediately looked down at the English muffin he was buttering. "The rain has to stop some time," she said with an edge to her voice she was unable to control. "Anyway, this family has plenty of social conscience without me." She took another sip of her father's coffee and then stood up. "See you later," she said to him. Without looking back at her mother, Amanda left the kitchen.

As she climbed the wide, curving stairs, she berated herself. She had done it again. Why couldn't she get through half an hour with her mother anymore without some kind of fight? It wasn't that she intended to be unpleasant. And she didn't want to be bored, either. But everything her mother suggested was worse than staying home. The idea of volunteering at the hospital was appalling. Imagine spending hours pushing a cart of candy bars around the smelly halls. Or worse, doing the terrible jobs the nurses didn't want to do. And then what would she do when the sun finally did come out, and she was stuck all day inside? She might as well take a job. At least, then, she'd have money to show for it. Not that she needed money, particularly. The only problem was the damned rain! Her mother had never bugged her about spending her summers on the river before. And when the sun was out, when all the kids could get out on the boats, it would probably be fun to be with Steve again, too. Then her mother could go back to focusing on her million mayor's-wife obligations and let Amanda alone. It was just the damned rain!

"Mandy!" Doug had almost walked into her as he came out of his room. "What are you doing up at this hour?"

Amanda ruffled her brother's auburn hair. "I could ask you the same thing. I thought you'd finally learned the joys of sleeping late."

He held up a bulging canvas bag. "Today's a work day," he said. "I'm going collecting at the Richmond Road cut. You want to come?"

"My dear brother, you know how I feel about fossils. If they let me alone, I'll let them alone. Anyway, it's raining. As usual."

"That's okay. In fact, that's good. The rain will have washed out a whole new batch of specimens by now." Doug wrinkled his thoroughly freckled face. "You ought to come with me, Mandy. You'd see. It's a lot more interesting than 'The Guiding Light.'"

Amanda put both hands around her brother's throat. "If people don't stop telling me what to do with my life, I'm going to do something desperate!"

"Watch it! I'm an undercover black belt. These hands are lethal weapons. Anyway, I'm hungry. Let go."

Amanda watched Doug take the steps two at a time, his collecting bag bouncing against the backs of his legs, and wished, as usual, that she had even half as much sense of herself at sixteen as Doug had at ten. She went into her room and sat down on her chintz-covered window seat. The rain on the turret windows blurred the view out over River Road and the trees below it to the Ohio River, now rushing by, carrying the debris of the unseasonable flood. Everything looked washed out, shades of gray, of green, of muddy brown. Any other year she'd be up at this hour too, but she'd be busy packing a lunch for herself and Steve, filling a canvas bag with towels and thongs and suntan lotion, her hairbrush, and a couple of decks of cards. The day would

4

stretch out in front of her full of waterskiing, lying on the beach where all the other kids would have tied up their boats, eating, listening to music, maybe later going down river to the marina with the new game room and dance floor. She did have a sense of herself, she decided. And a passion nearly as strong as Doug's for fossils. Her passion was for boats. And the river.

And why should she feel guilty about that? It was vacation, after all. She worked hard at school all year, didn't she? Hadn't summer vacation been created to give kids a chance to be kids? Just because Doug was ten going on thirty-five, did she have to be sixteen going on forty? Why was she supposed to want to do the same things with her life that her mother did? Anyway, what did her mother do that was so wonderful—besides look gorgeous and give speeches about beautifying Grantsport? Even if Julie had decided to take a job this year, why shouldn't the rest of them have a summer like other summers? Except that the weather wasn't cooperating. Nobody would be bugging her if she could only get out on the boat first thing in the morning. She wouldn't be around to bug.

Steve loved the river too, of course. It was part of what made the two of them such a perfect couple. Besides the fact that they lived only a few houses away from each other on River Road and that their fathers worked together. James Sterling, mayor of Grantsport, and William Randolph, city councilman, had been friends and law partners before Amanda and Steve had been old enough to be more than playmates. Stephen Randolph was a year older than Amanda, and a full three inches taller than her five nine. He had blond, wavy hair, blue eyes, a smile guaranteed to melt the heart. He was on the school's tennis team, had been president of his class for two years in a row and was always on the honor roll. Perfect.

5

But lately something had changed. Amanda didn't know exactly what it was, or when it had happened. Maybe it really was the pinball. He'd been on the pinball craze ever since his father had given him a machine for his seventeenth birthday. Amanda could not seem to get excited about pinball. Standing for hours, flipping those plastic flippers, even if it was free, seemed an unutterable waste. If not of money, then of time. Of life! Steve was a purist. When other guys played the electronic space games, he stood firm for pinball. His machine wasn't one of the small ones built to be played at home, but a genuine rebuilt classic, dating from the fifties. It didn't make electronic shrieks and laser whines, it had "authentic sound," as he called it. Even when they went to movies lately, Amanda would find herself either waiting while Steve played a commercial pinball game, or having to listen to another of his diatribes against people who had put in space games but didn't include pinball.

Amanda hadn't tried to explain any of this to her mother. Peg Sterling wouldn't be able to understand why something as insignificant as pinball could damage an otherwise perfect relationship. Or what looked like a perfect relationship. Her mother could see only the surface. When she looked at Steve she saw the wavy hair, the grades, the good family, the fact that he planned to study law. The Peg Sterling whose clothes were always perfect, whose makeup was in place before breakfast, whether she planned to leave the house or not, whose hair was never just combed, but always coiffed, quite naturally wanted her daughter to be seen with Stephen Randolph. Whether her daughter wanted that or not, Amanda thought. She watched a single drop of rain as it slid erratically down the windowpane, making its own path, then mingling with others.

6

If this were a normal summer, Amanda decided, she and her mother would not have this problem over Stephen. When he wasn't hunched over a pinball machine, after all, he was fun to be with. He had a good sense of humor, he really seemed to care about her, and—unlike a lot of the guys—he never pressured her to get more involved with him than she wanted to. When she was being fair, she had to admit that her mother could hardly be blamed for not understanding what was wrong between them. Amanda didn't understand it herself. There were a lot of things she didn't understand lately.

She leaned her forehead against the window and watched a huge tree float past on the river, half its roots pointing grotesquely at the sky. She felt like that. Uprooted and drifting. But why? There hadn't been a flood in her life. What could have undermined her roots?

Her father knocked on her open door and she turned away from the window. He had snugged his tie up to his shirt collar and buttoned his vest. He didn't look at all like a politician, Amanda thought. Standing in her doorway, grinning at her, his blue eyes twinkling, he looked like a cigarette-ad cowboy, dressed for some reason in a three-piece suit instead of jeans. His rugged good looks, the deeply etched lines in his face, even his thick brown hair, gave him the look of a man who worked outdoors rather than in an office. Except that this year he didn't have the tan he usually had by now from the weekends on the boat. "Don't let the rain get you down too much," he said. "Or your mother, either. I suspect she goes for Steve a little herself. She likes to have him around, anyway."

"He *is* a little young, don't you think?"

"Possibly. Besides, she has me. What more could a woman ask?"

Amanda went to her father and threw her arms around his neck. "Nothing," she said, and kissed his cheek. "Maybe that's my problem. Maybe I have an Oedipus complex."

"Electra complex, I think."

"Right. So I'm Electra." She kissed him again. "Have a good day."

"You too. And don't make such a face. I'll put out a decree that the rain has to stop. Okay?"

"Okay."

"Meantime, do me a favor, will you, love? Try to be a little nicer to your mother, even if you feel she's pressuring you. It's been a hard year for all of us. Especially for her."

"Why especially for her?" There he went again. Why was he always so solicitous of his wife? She didn't need it as far as Amanda could tell. And what had been so hard about the year anyway? The trouble had all blown over, hadn't it? No permanent damage had been done to any of them.

"Because your mother depends on having certain stable and permanent things in her life. When anything rocks the boat, it's particularly hard for her."

Amanda didn't believe it for a moment. Why did men think of women as fragile? Her mother was anything but! Anyway, if Peg Sterling did need stable and permanent things in her life, that was no excuse to keep everyone else from changing anything. Didn't the rest of them count at all? Besides, it wasn't as if she'd been picking fights with her mother. They seemed to happen in spite of her. Her father was looking at her, his face serious. "All right. I'll try."

"That's all I ask, kiddo. Good-bye."

"Bye."

Amanda watched her father's dark blue BMW inch down the steep driveway and turn left onto River Road before she put on her jeans and T-shirt. Then she sat in front of her mirror, combing her straight brown hair. Her face owed much to her father. It was long, strong boned, plain. On her father, it was great. But a rugged, honest face wasn't exactly what she would have chosen for herself. Her only obvious legacy from her mother was the light sprinkling of freckles across her straight nose. She wished she had inherited instead the petite frame, the creamy complexion, the vibrant auburn hair with the natural wave Doug had managed to get. Or best of all, the deep green eyes. Her own were almost completely nondescript. On her driver's license she had wondered what to put down under color. Sometimes they seemed blue, sometimes hazel. Finally, she had written "gray." Gray eyes, like the wretched rainy sky. Genes weren't fair. A reporter had called her "statuesque" once. Not bad, she supposed. But hardly "gorgeous" as people regularly called her mother. Was she jealous? Amanda put her comb down and stood up. Maybe of her looks, a little. But otherwise, no. Definitely not!

Doug was still in the kitchen when she went back downstairs, a huge book open on the table next to him, reading as he ate an English muffin with marmalade. From the crumbs around him, she assumed it was his third or fourth muffin. "Hey, Mandy," he said around his mouthful, "would you get me some more milk? Please?"

"What is this, glass number five?"

"Just the third. I'm a growing boy."

She poured the milk, shaking her head. "If you put all this food into growing, you're going to be ten feet tall by your twelfth birthday."

"There are many ways to grow, dear sister." He patted the book. "It takes energy to read, learn, and inwardly digest this stuff."

"Did you leave a muffin for me to inwardly digest?"

"Nope. Sorry. Not a thawed one—I think there are some in the freezer."

"I wish Mom would get over her fear of microwaves!" she said.

"She may be right about that, Mandy. We're always messing with stuff we don't really understand. Did you know that microwaves . . ."

"Never mind. I'll just have coffee."

Doug frowned. "You aren't doing anything dumb like dieting, are you?"

"Why? Do you think I need to?"

"Of course not. But that doesn't always mean anything."

"Don't worry. I'm not that type. I have no intention of starving myself. But with a locust like you in the house, the rest of us could starve by accident."

Doug closed his book and popped the last of his muffin into his mouth. "What're you doing today?"

Amanda looked out the window over the sink. Still gray. Still the rain streaming down the glass. "Nothing much. Why?"

"Just thought you might like to give me a ride out to the Richmond Road cut."

"What'll you do if I don't?"

"I could always hitch."

"Dad would kill you."

"To tell you the truth, I was planning to have Mom take me. I forgot she had a Junior League luncheon today. She has to wash her hair."

"Junior League? I thought after forty you're too old for that."

"She's their speaker. You know—urban art."

"Okay, I'll take you," Amanda said. At least it would give her something to do away from the house. "I suppose that means I get to pick you up, too."

10

"You could always stay there with me. Four eyes are better . . ."

"You're impossible! I told you, there are a million things I'd rather do than stand in the rain looking for prehistoric clams."

"Such as?" Peg Sterling came into the kitchen, carrying an emerald silk blouse on a hanger, a cream-colored linen suit over her arm.

Amanda shrugged. "Well, I thought I'd take some canned goods over to the Red Cross to help with flood relief, and then maybe roll some bandages. After that, maybe I'll save the whales . . ."

"Okay, okay." Peg Sterling pulled the ironing board down from its cupboard next to the refrigerator. "Make fun of social conscience all you want, Amanda. But there are better things to do than watch television or sleep."

"I know," Amanda said. She bit down her urge to ask what painting murals on the walls of downtown buildings had to do with saving the world. She watched her mother plug in the iron and check to be sure the setting was low enough. Cream linen and emerald silk. Her mother would be her usual perfect, elegant self when she spoke to the Junior League.

"Do you have a lunch packed?" Peg Sterling asked Doug.

"Does it rain in June?" Doug replied. "It's me, Mom. The eating machine. I've never forgotten to take a lunch in my life."

"Just checking. Some people are more careful about their nutrition than others."

Amanda placed a careful smile across her face. She'd been hungry when she came down to the kitchen. But now she would just make do with coffee. If it wasn't one thing it was another. And if not direct, then sideways and sarcastic. What was really bothering her mother, anyway?

11

Was it just that Amanda didn't feel like being with Steve right now? She stood up. "I'll go get my keys," she said to Doug. "Be ready when I come back down, okay?"

Doug grinned. "Sure. I just have to get my rain gear on."

Amanda ran up the stairs to get her purse from her room. If she didn't get out of the house and away from her mother, they'd be right in the middle of it again, no matter what she'd told her father. This wasn't about social conscience at all, she thought. Because if she and Steve were going out on the river every day, her mother wouldn't be hassling her, even though their being out in the boats did no one any good except themselves. In fact, if Peg Sterling were really so concerned about larger moral issues, she wouldn't want them using all that gasoline for fun. Social conscience was a smoke screen, a way to cover up her manipulation.

Her mother never seemed to worry about what Stephen was doing for the world. She wouldn't expect him to do volunteer work. Peg Sterling didn't mind his playing pinball or tennis. Amanda couldn't see what made going to a movie better, more "moral," than watching television. Maybe it was enough for Steve just to *be*. Maybe he could goof off now because eventually he'd be a lawyer, or a politician like her father. Or maybe it was just that he was male. Amanda grinned at her reflection in the mirror as she picked up her purse from her dresser. Maybe Peg Sterling was a male chauvinist. Wouldn't that accusation send her up the wall?

The trouble with her mother's life, Amanda thought, was that it was a life of images. Gorgeous mayor's wife. Happy mayor's family. She and Steve fit nicely as long as they preserved their perfect-couple image. Now that Amanda was disrupting that, she was disrupting her relationship with her mother as well. So what kind of a relationship was it, then? And why should she be the one to feel guilty about all this bickering? She hadn't started it, after all.

· 2 ·

Amanda did a tight U-turn and drove back past Doug, his yellow-slickered figure looking small and lonely against the huge gray cliff of the Richmond Road cut. He put down his bag and waved as she passed him. In her rear-view mirror, she noted that before the road curved and took her out of sight, he was already stooped over, picking up and discarding bits of rock.

What intrigued him so about fossils was more than she could understand. She had listened to any number of his lectures, as he pointed out perfect specimens among his collection, so carefully sorted and packed into egg carton after egg carton. Half his room was devoted to his fossil collection, the books about fossils, his collecting and label-ing gear. She had asked him once how he could get excited by an ancient world in which the highest form of life was a kind of squid. "Can't you imagine it?" he'd asked her. "That warm, shallow ocean, with all those animals? Even the crinoids—that look like water lillies, sort of—even those were animals. Right here, right where this house is, the water and sand and sunlight, the moss animals and the cephalopods swimming among them, the crinoids moving in the waves, trilobites—right here! Four hundred and fifty million years ago! Can't you imagine it?"

Amanda had had to admit that she couldn't imagine it,

or if she could, if she could call up a picture in her mind of an ocean like that, it didn't stir any interest in her any more than she could get herself interested in the bottom of the river, in crayfish or catfish or the ungainly, big-scaled carp. Those, too, interested Doug, but less than fossils. He'd catch turtles at the marina sometimes, or crayfish, and keep them for a while in the huge aquarium that lived in his room, empty for most of the year, feeding them minnows he netted. But he always let them go after a short time. A living, breathing animal was less wonderful to him than the intricate rock forms of animals dead for hundreds of millions of years.

His obsession had begun when he was only five. Peg Sterling had been serving on the board of the county historical society and, not having a baby-sitter one day, had taken him with her to a lecture by a paleontologist from Cincinnati. Doug had come home glowing with a new, mad enthusiasm. Already he had learned some of the wonderful new words. He had pointed out, between the garage and the back porch, that the flagstones were masses of brachiopods and bryozoans. Amanda envied Doug his obsession a little. While knowing where your life was going might lessen the adventure a little, it would lessen the confusion, too.

Not that life had been all that easy for Doug so far. Once he'd begun to learn about fossils, anything that forced him in any other direction made him crazy with impatience. He would cheerfully learn chemistry, history, geology, *any* subject that could be related to paleontology in any way. But he treated any other kind of education as a desperate waste of time. Kindergarten, she remembered, had driven him nearly insane. "Cutting and coloring and singing little songs," he would rage, his small face screwed up in frustration. "Nothing in the whole room to read!"

He could already read, of course, was comfortable with words like "gastropod" and "*Platystrophia*." For him, reading was a tool rather than an end in itself, so first grade, with its little cards, each lettered with one tiny word, had sometimes made him literally sick. Adults, especially his teachers, had not known what to do with this little boy who announced with grave seriousness that he intended to be a paleontologist and didn't need the first grade at all. Only his being the mayor's son had kept him from spending his life in the principal's office. No one seemed to understand that his impatience with school was genuine, inevitable. The other grades had not suited him any better, of course. As his knowledge had become more sophisticated, his distance from the materials of the classroom had grown.

He had had few friends of his own age, ever. None of the other kids could relate to his all-consuming interest in the Ordovician age, and the very idea of playing with matchbox cars or pretending to be the captain of a spaceship had always bored him silly. For a while the Sterlings had tried to convince him that having friends his own age was important, but they had at last given up. He seemed content with his own company, corresponded regularly with the paleontologist who had first turned him on to fossils, and was the only child member of a local amateur group that often went on collecting trips. When Peg Sterling sometimes mourned her son's lost childhood, Doug only laughed at her. "I *am* a child, Mom. Honest. Just look how short I am." Then he would make a face. "I can prove I'm a child! Who else could be forced to spend three-quarters of every year in a classroom?"

Amanda grinned into the blur of the windshield. Her friends who had younger brothers or sisters seemed barely to tolerate them. But Doug was something else. Brilliant,

16

funny, downright nice—and incredibly stubborn. No matter what the punishment, he continued to skip school in the spring and fall when the weather was perfect for collecting. Again, being the son of the mayor kept him out of serious trouble. And since he refused to concern himself with grades, his teachers had no hold over him at all. Peg Sterling raged at him for his truancy, but their father had finally given up on that too, and tolerated his behavior with a kind of exasperated good will. Doug can't help it that he's different, Amanda thought, and wondered as usual how Doug had turned out the way he did, when she was so utterly conventional herself.

As the world alternately cleared and blurred behind her windshield wipers, Amanda found herself driving more slowly. She had agreed to take Doug to his collecting site, but that was as far as her plans for the day had gone. She didn't know where she was going now. She didn't want to go home. Her mother would be there, putting the final touches on her hair and makeup, checking the full-length mirror for the perfect combination of accessories, perhaps going over her speech. She did that in the mirror too, though Amanda couldn't imagine why she would have to work at the speech. She'd already given it half a dozen times. In a city the size of Grantsport, she had to be careful or she'd give the same speech to the same people over and over. This time it was the "urban art" project, trying to raise the money to commission murals for the sides of downtown buildings. Other times it was the establishment of a recycling center, or a campaign to restore historical buildings, or the creation of a downtown shopping area banned to cars, paved with brick, and planted with trees and gardens and fountains. Peg Sterling took her position far more seriously than the other local political wives. Steve's mother, for instance, might just as well be married to a shoe salesman. She was a broad, comfortable woman fond of bridge and trading grocery coupons. There had been a time when June Randolph and her mother had been friends, but that seemed long ago now. It was certainly before the talk began of James Sterling's running for governor.

If James Sterling became governor, if they all went to live in Columbus, Peg Sterling could broaden her efforts to include the whole state. She would probably decide to make Ohio the "garden state" of the Midwest. During the winter, when the hysteria over the collapsed gym roof had been at its height, the mayor in the center of it all, when the talk of the governorship had abruptly stopped, Peg Sterling had become a whirlwind. She had gone from group to group with the enthusiasm she usually devoted to a re-election campaign, reminding Grantsport citizens of the many accomplishments of their mayor. She had cited the statistics about the city's mass-transportation system—the best for a city of its size in the state, in several states. She had focused on the downtown renewal her husband had spearheaded, the development of the riverfront, her own success in getting buildings put on the national register. She had been a one-woman pep rally, rolling over the rumors and unpleasantness like a steamroller. It was readily admitted at city hall that she had been a major factor in the dying down of the furor and the reemergence of her husband's prospects for the governorship.

Amanda wasn't sure what there was in that mayor's-wife stance that bothered her so. Maybe it was that her mother seemed almost to care more about her husband's position than about him, more about her chances of becoming a governor's wife than about his reputation. Amanda was having trouble lately knowing when her mother truly meant what she said and when she was speaking for effect. No, she didn't want to go home until she was sure her mother was safely off to that meeting.

Julie would be working, Kit would be somewhere with Mark. She reached over and turned on the radio, set for some reason to Steve's favorite rock station. Steve didn't ride in her car very much. He preferred to drive his own car when they went out. Amanda suspected it was jealousy. When her father had handed her the keys to her car on her sixteenth birthday, she had run out to the garage and then stood stunned at the sight of the small white car gleaming as pale as the moon next to her mother's station wagon. The carriage house–garage, big enough for three cars, had always seemed cavernous. With the Datsun 280ZX in the extra space, the size seemed just right. "I had to get you something small," her father had said, pretending apology, "so there would still be room for the bikes and the lawn mower."

Stephen's car, a two-year-old Camaro Z28, had been his pride and joy until he had seen hers. Then he had joked about how small hers was, complained at the new-car smell, and decided it wasn't right for a girl to drive on a date. He had ridden with her only a few times. Julie and Kit had both loved the car and sometimes they'd gone driving, ignoring the crush of the three of them in a two-seater, showing it off. But by now the excitement had worn off. There was no place to drive it really fast, and Amanda wasn't sure she liked the idea of driving fast anyway. The roar of power was gratifying when she pulled away from a traffic light, but even that was not as wonderful as it had been at first because of the constant realization that she couldn't really use all the power the car could produce. That was probably the difference between the way she felt about driving and the way she felt at the wheel of the boat. The Peg o' My Heart could be run full out, its speed and

19

power cutting through the waves. There was the wind in her face, the rise and fall as she took the boat over the heavy wake of a barge. Those sensations were impossible to duplicate on land.

The Peg was her passion, all right. And the river. The first time her father had let her take the boat out on her own, she had been overwhelmed by the sense of freedom. If she wanted to, she could just keep going, down the Ohio River, eventually all the way to the Gulf of Mexico. She'd never been far on her own, of course. The cost of gas was more than even her ample allowance could bear. It wasn't a practical thing, this free feeling. But the openness of the river, the movement of it, lured her. A boat on a lake would be boring, with nowhere to go except around and around. On the river, she could go places—down to Cincinnati, up, even all the way to Pittsburgh. And there were the tributaries, a whole network of waterways theoretically linking her to most of the Midwest. Like Huckleberry Finn, she always felt on the river the option of leaving. And in the Peg, she would be leaving with not only power and speed under her hands, but a comfortable place to live going with her. All she'd have to do would be to tie up along the bank, cook meals, sleep in her comfortable bunk.

That was it. It might be raining, and the river level might be too high for boating, but she could at least spend the afternoon on the Peg. No one would think of looking for her at the marina in this weather, so she wouldn't even have to think about Steve or her mother. And there was no phone. She could get some lunch at the marina coffee shop, and she had put some paperbacks she hadn't read yet under her bunk. The electricity was on. In fact, the Peg offered the coziest, most isolated haven she could think of. So when she turned onto River Road, she passed Stephen's house, then her own, and turned into the marina parking lot.

She locked the car, leaving her purse under her seat, and slipped the keys into her raincoat pocket. It was strange to see the marina so deserted this late in June. The only people today seemed to be up at the boat sales building where a few cars were parked near the door. Even the coffee shop looked empty. The water of Ryan Creek, the marina's access to the river, was turbid, its surface littered with sticks, leaves, cans, dead fish, and the miscellaneous debris always gathered up by a flood and pushed to the shores and into quieter waters. The boat launching ramp was half-submerged, and the wooden gangways that connected the floating docks to the roadways were almost level instead of angling sharply down to the surface of the creek. Rain was still coming down steadily from the fat gray blobs of clouds overhead. By the time she had reached the main dock, walking carefully on the slippery wood, Amanda's jeans and jogging shoes were soaked.

The Peg was moving gently on the muddy, rain-spotted water, her fat white bumpers thudding softly against the wooden slip. The new canvas over her back deck was clean and taut. The gold letters, "Peg o' My Heart, Grantsport, Ohio," gleamed against the mahogany of her stern. Stephen's family had bought a new fiberglass cruiser a few years before to avoid the constant care required by wooden boats. But James Sterling had kept the Peg. "She takes a little extra care," he'd said, "but she's worth every bit of it. What's worth having is worth working for." Each year he had her hull scraped and painted, but he lovingly cared for her bright work himself. Amanda loved the feel of the red leather of the seats, loved the smell of the cabin, a waxy, woody smell that took her back to her earliest childhood when she'd been able to lie in the point of the front

21

bunk and look up through the open hatch at the blue of the sky overhead. Sometimes, when she had been supposedly taking a nap, her mother had looked down from her sunbathing spot on the deck to find Amanda looking back, wide awake. Her mother would just laugh and toss Amanda a pretzel or a piece of fruit.

Amanda walked out onto the finger of dock and stood next to the bow. There were so many memories associated with the Peg. The summers when they had taken long trips on her, the weekends when they had tied up along the banks of one of the tributaries. Sometimes the Sterlings had gone alone, other times they had gone with the Randolphs, or with Kit's family, tying the boats up together for dinners cooked over open fires on the beach. Kit's parents had had a houseboat, so when it rained on a weekend trip, they would all gather in the "Dream Castle" where the adults played cards and the older kids played Monopoly or Chinese checkers. It had been different then. Each family had been a unit and the whole group had been such good friends. A family could hardly avoid being close when they shared the cabin of a twenty-two-foot cruiser. Everyone had a job. Even when Doug was tiny, he had been in charge of stowing dry towels, life jackets, books, and games in the appropriate lockers under the bunks. It had been Amanda's job as soon as she was old enough to make up the bunks at bedtime, and in the morning to air the sleeping bags and stow them, to return the bunks to their daytime jobs as seats for the table.

It had all changed when the older kids could drive the boats themselves. By then, Kit's parents were divorced and they had sold the houseboat. After that, Kit had usually come with Amanda on the Peg. The weekend trips had dwindled to a few each summer because everyone seemed to have Saturday commitments and they could no longer take off every Friday evening. The cruisers had become ski boats, picnic boats, day-trippers for the kids on weekdays. Only occasionally did anyone take longer trips anymore. And almost never did the families go in groups. Amanda missed the old ways, sometimes, but the truth was that she preferred driving the Peg now to riding on her, and the company of the other kids to the families. She wished she could take the Peg out today. She kicked at the dock cleat to which the boat was tied.

"The rain isn't *her* fault!"

Amanda jumped, startled by the sudden voice behind her. She turned and saw a boy at the junction of the main dock and the finger. He was about Stephen's age, tall and angular, but his shoulders were broad. He looked as if he might be stronger than his build suggested. He was dressed in dirty jeans, a black T-shirt, and a tattered army-fatigue jacket, which hung open, its pockets bulging with apparently heavy objects. He wore no hat, and his too-long black hair was plastered against his forehead by the rain. He was smiling at her in a way that seemed at once both admiring and mocking. He looked like one of the guys who worked at the marina, but she'd never seen him before. She thought she knew all of them.

"You startled me," she said, realizing that he knew it perfectly well, having seen her jump like that at the sound of his voice.

"Sorry." He didn't say anything further, just stood there, looking at her.

"Who are you?" she asked.

"I could ask you the same thing." He kept looking at her steadily, and Amanda began to feel uncomfortable under his scrutiny. She couldn't remember ever having

23

been stared at this way—so openly, and from such close range. It began to feel like some kind of attack. As if his eyes were weapons. Her hands felt suddenly large and clumsy, and she couldn't think what to do with them. Finally, she put them into the pockets of her raincoat and stared back at him. But she wasn't used to this kind of duel, and dropped her eyes to the dock. His shoes, she noted, were black basketball shoes, worn through at the sides. He wore no socks. The sight of his skin through the tattered canvas embarrassed her and she looked back at his face to meet that constant, insolent stare.

"Well?" he said.

"Well, what?" She felt goosebumps rising on her arms and realized that she was frightened. What might he have in those pockets? She was glad she had left her purse in the car. She glanced around, hoping to see someone, to reassure herself that she wasn't alone here with this person.

"Are you going to introduce yourself? Or maybe I should just ask if that's your boat you're mooning over."

Amanda put her hand protectively on the Peg's deck. "Of course she's mine. My family's." His face didn't change. He must have known that already, she thought. "But I asked first. Who are *you*? I haven't seen you around here before." Her voice, despite her attempt to make it casual, came out tight, its pitch too high.

"I haven't been around here before." He set his feet more firmly and folded his arms across his chest. "So you're the one."

"What one?"

"The daughter of the infamous Mayor Sterling." He smiled, and this time the smile seemed only mocking. "The description I heard doesn't do you justice. Definitely not."

"What is that supposed to mean—'infamous'?"

24

"Don't tell me you don't know the meaning of the word!"

"I know what it means. Why did you call my father infamous?"

"I should think you'd know perfectly well why. I may be new around here, but even I've heard about the gym roof. Your father's gym roof."

Anger welled up and overcame whatever fear Amanda had been feeling. She took a step toward him, her hands clenched into fists. She had a wild impulse to punch this guy in the mouth. "It was not my father's gym roof! He had nothing to do with the fact that it fell. All that talk was over months ago. If you're new here, I can't imagine where you even got that story."

"I got the 'story,' if that's what you want to call it, from my Uncle Frank. I guess he forgot to tell me it wasn't true."

"Your uncle Frank? Frank Essig? The man who owns this marina?"

"Sorry," he said. The voice was anything but apologetic. "I forgot to introduce myself. Joe Schmidt. Frank and Myra are my uncle and aunt. I'm working here for the summer."

Amanda felt herself relax a little. At least he had a legitimate reason for being here. She noted the dirt under his fingernails, the grease on his jacket. He looked like one of the mechanics because he was one. And no matter how unpleasant he was, at least if he were related to Frank and Myra, he probably wasn't actually dangerous. "I'm surprised that anyone related to Frank Essig could be so—so rude," she said. She wished she had been able to think of something stronger to say. "Rude" sounded wrong, somehow. Silly.

25

"I guess I'm from the wrong side of the family. We Schmidts are weak on manners. At least I've introduced myself, which is more than I can say for you."

"You made it quite clear that you already know who I am."

"Ah, yes. But I'm new, remember? I don't know your first name. I suppose you do have a first name? 'Miss Sterling' seems a little too formal for this setting."

"My name is Amanda." He stepped toward her and held out his right hand. The distance between them now was only inches, it seemed. She had an impulse to step back, but fought it down. She was not going to give him the satisfaction. She took his hand. "Amanda. Amanda Sterling." He said her name slowly, as if testing it against some memory or internal expectation. "Amanda. That fits, I think." The palm of his hand was hard, his grip firm, almost painful. His dark eyes were fixed intently on her face. Amanda could feel her cheeks getting warm. The rain was suddenly cold against her face. "Amanda means 'worthy of love,' doesn't it?"

Amanda swallowed against the sudden constriction in her throat. "Yes," she said, her voice barely audible. She pulled her hand away and put it back into her pocket.

"I've made something of a study of names, actually," he said. "Names and engines. A vast range of knowledge, don't you think?" He laughed a short, dry laugh. "Well, Amanda Sterling, it's been nice chatting with you this way. Here on the dock in this lovely weather. But I really do have to get back to work. If we don't have all these floating hotels ready by the time the rain stops and the river goes down, their owners might be inconvenienced. And God knows we wouldn't want to see anyone inconvenienced!" He stepped back against the side of the Peg, leaving a way past him. "No doubt you want to get back to your nice dry 280ZX."

The dock was so narrow that Amanda had to brush against him to get past. She held her breath, aware that her heart seemed to be beating double time. She was afraid he might grab her, push her, something. But he stood as if unaware that she had touched him. She forgot her intention to spend the afternoon on the Peg as she hurried down the main dock.

"Be careful!" his mocking voice called after her. "These docks are slippery when they're wet."

As if she didn't know that as well as he did. When she stepped off the gangway, it was all she could do to keep from breaking into a run. At the car, she jerked at the door, forgetting she had locked it. Sheepishly, aware that he was still standing there, watching her, she took her keys from her pocket, unlocked the door, slipped in and slammed it. When she tried to put the key into the ignition, she saw that her hand was shaking. Who did he think he was, anyway? And how could he possibly be related to the Essigs? In all the years the Peg had been docked at the Essigs' marina, they had never been anything but friendly and helpful. What had Frank Essig told his nephew about her father?

She started the car, turned the radio up as if to drown out her thoughts, and shifted into reverse. The car leaped backward. She shoved it into first and roared out of the parking lot, skidding wildly on the gravel as she took off. Maybe it was a good day for a drive after all.

·3·

Joe stood, watching Amanda. He smiled when she jerked at her car door and fumbled for her keys. The car's skidding departure made him smile again. As he walked back to the houseboat he'd been working on, he had a pang of guilt. What had he done that for? It certainly hadn't been his intention when he'd followed Amanda Sterling down here, to do one of his numbers on her. That was unworthy, he told himself roughly. But there it was. He hadn't been able to help himself. Something in the way she had reacted to him had triggered it as surely as the scent of blood triggered a shark attack. Jekyll and Hyde, he told himself. One minute he could be a perfectly reasonable, nice guy, and the next he could find himself enjoying watching some rich kid squirm. He certainly ought to know better—did know better. He ought to have better control. That was it.

He picked his way around the engine cover and lowered himself into the well next to the engine. Having stood on the dock in the rain like a madman, he had managed to get himself soaked to the skin. And even though it wasn't cold out, he'd be chilled through if he worked in wet clothes the rest of the morning. He could go back to the houseboat and change into dry clothes, of course, but he decided against it. Wet clothes would be a fitting punishment for the way he had treated Amanda Sterling. As he picked up the socket wrench, he smiled again.

It wasn't the first time he'd played the game. He'd known all his life, it seemed, about the way rich kids looked at him. The way they took in his clothes, placed him neatly below themselves, and then proceeded to look through him. As if he didn't exist. Or if he did, that he must be there to do them some sort of service. At the garage where his brother worked he had seen it often enough. When people brought in classy cars to be worked on, they didn't really see the guy who did the work. They wouldn't even know, when they came in to pick up the car, who they had talked to before. It was the moment when, having placed him, they dismissed him—it was that moment that triggered his hostility. Worse yet was his certainty that they assumed not only that they were richer than he, but that they were smarter. People always seemed to think money and intelligence went together. That, he couldn't stand.

He couldn't remember when he first discovered his power over rich kids. It was so simple, really, and the results were always so gratifying. All he had to do was break their rules, step out of the place they had made for him. Sometimes, particularly with the girls, all he had to do was stare. It was astonishing. He could just stand there and stare into their faces, and they would get scared. Probably it worked because they'd been taught that it wasn't polite to stare, they'd been told that from the cradle on, and nobody in their world would do such a thing. It was a rule. If someone came along who looked different, didn't dress properly, and broke one of their rules, there was no telling what he might do. Blocking a girl's way—on the sidewalk or a stairway—was another good one. If she let him know she wanted to get by him and he didn't immediately move,

29

there was that flicker of fear. As if it might be only one tiny step from refusing to move to pulling out a machine gun and mowing down everyone in sight. They were terrified that the bad, unpredictable world might suddenly invade their carefully ordered lives.

There was something different about this girl, he admitted to himself, but he couldn't be sure how much was a real difference in her and how much was in him. He had seen the car pull into the parking lot from the window of the coffee shop, where he was finishing a cup of coffee with his aunt. His first thought when she stepped out was disgust that anyone so young would have a car that cost so much, so obviously new, so obviously hers. He had watched her lock her door and start down toward the dock, and it had been then that he'd noticed whatever it was about her that had made him follow her. It wasn't that she was pretty. How could anyone tell what she looked like in a raincoat with the hood up. It had something to do with the way she carried herself, the way she moved. She was tall, but instead of slumping slightly, the way most tall girls did, she seemed proud of her height. Or perhaps not proud, just comfortable with it. Comfortable with herself, who she was and how she looked. Maybe, he reflected, working to loosen a rusted spark plug, maybe it was having been raised the daughter of a small city's mayor. She'd been raised to think she was somebody, and it probably never occurred to her to wonder if it were true or not. He had put down his coffee cup and called to his aunt, who was busy at something behind the counter, that he was going back to work. And he had followed, not quite certain why he was following. Just to watch her, maybe with the thought of meeting her. Even now, he couldn't be sure which it had been, but one thing was certain—he'd had no intention of hassling her. It had probably been the sound

30

of the rain on the water that had kept her from hearing him until he was so close that he was afraid if she turned and saw him suddenly, she'd be frightened. So he'd spoken, and had frightened her anyway.

When she had turned to look at him, something happened. It was as if he'd been punched in the stomach or had taken hold of a hot wire. Whatever it was, it was right out of a song, or a romantic novel. Again, it wasn't that she was pretty. Her face was a little too long, a little too strong to be called pretty. Strands of hair had escaped her hood and lay against her prominent cheekbones. They made her look almost vulnerable, despite the strong features. And then there were the freckles. Not many, just a light sprinkling of rusty dots across the bridge of her nose. Joe had a long-standing weakness for freckles.

But after the first startled look she'd given him, he'd seen the other, the look that registered his appearance and relegated him immediately to his proper place. Below her. Outside her circle. Not to be taken seriously. And he had fallen into his old game without meaning to, as unable to stop himself as Mr. Hyde when the potion was working. So much for romantic novels and old songs.

And it had worked on her as it always worked. It had frightened her. He remembered with grim satisfaction her inability to counter his stare, that glance around as if for help, the tension in her voice. Until he had mentioned her father. What had he said, anyway? "Infamous." It had turned off the fear as if he'd thrown a switch. His uncle had mentioned the story, and it had sprung to Joe's mind for no particular reason, except as a way to get more of a psychological edge. Actually, his uncle had called it small potatoes as political scandals went. But it had certainly connected with her. There had been a moment there when he'd expected her to strike out at him. He had gotten off

31

the subject then. Anger hadn't been the reaction he'd wanted.

When he had offered to shake her hand it had been like touching the live wire again. Her hand had been cold, but soft, her fingers long and slim. He had suddenly been aware of his dirty fingernails, had gripped her hand hard. Probably too hard, judging from the way she'd pulled hers away. And then she'd brushed against him when she passed. He had had to grip the gunwhale of her boat then, feeling his heart pounding violently. Back to romantic novels.

Joe turned on the small portable radio at his side. He didn't like the music he could get on it and wished he could afford a decent FM radio, but it was better to endure the rock station with the mouthy disc jockey than to work all morning with that incessant drumming of rain on the canopy over his head. Anyway, it was time to get his mind off Amanda Sterling. The memory of her hand in his was not a memory he could afford. She was poison. If there was one thing he didn't need this summer, on top of everything else, it was to be put down by a girl. Someday things would be different. But for now, Amanda Sterling was out of his class. Anything else was just a dream, and he didn't have the time or energy to waste wishing things were different.

Joe Schmidt didn't have a 280ZX or a boat to visit in the rain. He had nothing, he told himself firmly, except himself and this job. And a mind he would keep sharp on his own, despite long days of boat engines and rain and rock music on a cheap radio. He didn't have a mayor for a father. He didn't have a father at all. He had made that choice, and it would have to be as firm as if it were really true. He didn't have a father at all.

The memory was trying to come back, bringing the dull

ache it always brought. Joe tried to concentrate on the movements of his hands changing spark plugs, to listen to the lyrics of the song on the radio, anything to keep the memory at bay. But nothing worked.

His father had been sitting at the table that January morning, his elbows on the red-and-white-checked plastic tablecloth, alternately biting into his toast and using it as a stopper for the eggs he was forking into his mouth. Joe had dumped cereal into a bowl and poured himself a cup of coffee. It was still half an hour before he had to leave for school. His older brother and his mother had already left—his brother to the garage he managed, his mother to the grocery store where she worked a check-out lane. Joe was the only Schmidt still in school. His sister had dropped out at sixteen to get married and have a baby. Now she lived two blocks away in a duplex shared with her husband's parents, and worked at the grocery while her mother-in-law watched the baby. At seventeen, Linda had already begun the life their mother had lived for twenty years.

"Pete left almost an hour ago," Carl Schmidt said, his mouth full of toast and eggs.

"Yeah, Dad. He always leaves before I do."

"You can't goof off when you're a manager. You gotta be there before everybody else." Joe sighed and bent over his cereal. It was going to be this conversation again. "You can't expect the rest of your life to be as easy as school."

"I know, Dad." There was no point in reminding his father that after graduation, only five months away now, there would be four more years of school and then maybe several more after that.

"Nobody else in this family eats food they don't help pay for."

Joe put his spoon down. Why was it he could never just

go on eating when his father said that? Why did his stomach immediately turn over? Didn't he have as much right to eat as anyone else?

"Pete was bringing in money to help pay the bills around here by the time he was sixteen."

"I'm going to make money, Dad."

His father gulped at his coffee and picked up another piece of toast, which he used like a sponge to clean the egg off his plate. "When? In four years? You're already eighteen."

"And I'm going to college."

"So you can get a job that makes a pile of money, huh?"

"Dad, we've had this talk before."

"Right. Only you never seem to listen to what I'm saying when we have this talk. Two years already you've been taking from this family without giving anything back. Two years more than your brother. Even two years more than Linda. And you want another four years because you're such a smart kid."

Joe pushed his chair away from the table. "I'm not asking you for anything. I'll get scholarships to pay for college. I won't be living at home. I won't be eating your food."

His father picked up an envelope that had been lying next to his plate. "You see this? This is from the financial-aid office at the school you want to go to."

"What is it?" Joe felt a constriction in his chest. What was coming here?

"It's a form they say I gotta fill out if you want your scholarship."

The Parent Financial Statement. He hadn't warned his father it would be coming; he hadn't had the nerve to bring it up yet.

34

"They say I got two weeks to fill this out and send it back. Have you seen it?"

Joe shook his head. He hadn't seen the form, but he knew what it was like. It required his father to record every aspect of the family's financial position. It also required a copy of part of last year's income tax return.

"They're asking me to tell them things nobody outside this family has any right to know."

"They want to be sure they give scholarships only to people who really need them," Joe said. "It's tax money, you know." His palms felt damp. He should have prepared his father for this somehow.

"Okay," his father said. "Okay. I see their point. I can see they don't want some kid driving a Mercedes Benz around campus and using our taxes to pay for his books."

Joe took a breath. Was it going to be all right after all?

"But I want to know something before I fill this thing out and tell a bunch of strangers everything about my family. I want to know what you're going to college *for*."

"We've been over that and over it."

"Suppose you tell me again."

"I want to go on with my education."

"You think Pete didn't go on with his education when he went to work at the garage? You think he didn't have to be plenty smart to go from youngest mechanic to manager in just four years working for a guy like Henderson?"

"I never said Pete wasn't smart."

"So what kind of education is it you expect to get in four more years of school? What is it you plan to learn?"

"Dad, I want to know things you can't find out working as a mechanic. I want to do something with my life that's different from what Pete's doing with his."

"And what I've done with mine, huh?" Carl Schmidt

put down the envelope he'd been holding up all this time and poured himself another cup of coffee. "Working on a line isn't good enough for you. And managing a business isn't either. You're going to school so you can be better than your family, isn't that right?"

"Not better, Dad. Different. I don't want the same things. I never have."

"You want to write, huh? Books. Poetry. Stuff like that."

"Yes."

"What kind of a living is that supposed to make?"

"If you mean how much money, I don't know. It depends on a lot of things."

"You know how much you could make as an engineer? Or an accountant? You know what kind of a living you could make with four years of some kind of sensible education? An education that would get you ready for some kind of job?"

"I want to major in English, Dad. In writing."

At that, his father had wiped his mouth on a paper napkin and stood up. "Well, here it is, Joey. If you major in English, you find a way to get your education without this form here. Because I'm not going to tell the world what kind of money problems we've got so you can spend tax money making sure you'll have worse problems. If you want me to fill out this form, you have to change your plans. You can go to college. You can spend four years learning something that'll give you some kind of future! I'm not telling you what to choose. There's plenty of things you could study. Just pick one. You've had these last two years of high school on me, on your brother, on your mother. Now you do something in return. You get yourself an education that'll pay. So that if your family needs your help someday, you'll be able to give it. I'm not asking so much. Take some English courses if you want. Write

36

whatever you want to write in your free time. But you major in English and I don't fill out this form. You major in English and you're on your own."

At that moment, it hadn't seemed so bad. Joe had been angry, really furious at the assumption that his father had a right to tell him to do something with his life he didn't want to do. It was his life, after all, and his brain and hard work that had gotten him grades good enough for scholarships, SATs so good that colleges had been practically begging him to enroll. The Parent Financial Statement couldn't be all that important. After all, it wasn't his father going to school. So that morning, as he'd left the house, Joe had been almost relieved. At least the eternal argument was over. His father had made his final statement, and Joe had made his. He would, of course, choose English.

But that was before he had called the Financial Aid Office at the university. That was before he discovered that without a Parent Financial Statement he wouldn't be eligible for a scholarship. He'd asked about student loans. The answer was the same. Federal loans were based on need; they, too, required a PFS. Perhaps he could find a bank somewhere, but the man he'd spoken to hadn't been optimistic. Banks required co-signers, and usually the co-signer for a student loan had to be a parent. Both parents. Further, the man had warned, most banks didn't like to make loans to freshmen, whose determination to finish an education hadn't been tested yet.

What was the alternative, he'd asked, if his father refused to fill out the form? The man had paused for a moment, and Joe imagined him wondering about a father who would refuse to fill out a form so his son could get a scholarship. When he had answered, the man had sounded discouraged. Almost no one, he warned, could prove independent status the year of high school graduation. There were three requirements. It had to be shown that the parents had not claimed the child as a dependent for two full tax years, that the child had not lived at home for more than six weeks in either year, nor had received more than $1,000 toward his or her support.

"Tax years?" Joe had asked. "You mean January to January?"

"That's right. So if you live at home until you graduate, you'll have made it impossible to count this calendar year."

Joe had asked about other possibilities, but they had been almost nonexistent. Some private scholarships might be available, the man had said, though they were usually quite small. Or a bank might be found that would take a chance on a freshman, provided he could get some powerful recommendations. Clearly, his grades and his test scores were adequate. But there would still be the problem of finding co-signers.

The man had been kind enough, seemed truly sorry about the situation. The university, he had assured Joe, would be proud to have him as a student, and he certainly hoped Joe would be able to find a way around his problem.

It was incredible. For most things, including voting for the President of the United States, an eighteen year old was considered an adult. But for getting an education, he was only his father's son. Dependent. Stuck. By nothing more than refusing to fill out a form, his father could keep him from going to college in the fall.

Joe briefly considered telling his father he would major in engineering, even enrolling as an engineering major, then changing to English once he'd started school. But that would only get him the first year, and he'd be back where he started. Besides, it was dishonest. No matter how unreasonable his father was being, he'd always been straight with Joe. He couldn't accept his father's terms, but he couldn't bring himself to lie to him either. If he had to work for two and a half years to avoid spending four years studying what he didn't want to study, he would just have to do that. No matter what, he was going to college, and he was going to be a writer!

Then he had tried to find a job. Unemployment was high in Greenburg, and unemployment among teen-agers was astronomical. He could have worked part-time at a hamburger stand until school was out, but the pay was ludicrous. He found a tutoring job thanks to his literature teacher, but it was scarcely more than pocket money, and would end when school ended. For weeks he combed the classified ads, without success. In the meantime, he was avoiding his father. If the state wanted him orphaned to qualify for financial aid, he would orphan himself. From now on, he told himself, I have no father. He would find a job and move out of the house, and that would be the end of that. Pete offered him part-time work at the garage, but he turned it down. He didn't want help from Pete, no matter how kindly offered.

Joe didn't know whether his mother had had anything to do with Uncle Frank's job offer, but by the time it had come along in May, he'd been desperate enough to take it without asking questions. He could no longer afford the luxury of spurning family help. Ironically, he was qualified for Uncle Frank's job because he was a Schmidt, because he had learned about engines, as Pete had, at his father's knee. As kids, they had both spent Saturdays with their father working on cars—sometimes it would be the family car, sometimes cars Carl Schmidt fixed for friends and neighbors. Their mother used to say they'd been born with silver wrenches in their mouths.

The whole family had come to see the first Schmidt ever to graduate. Joe had been valedictorian of his class. Most of the guys Joe had grown up with had either quit school or switched to vocational programs. A valedictorian from that crowd was unheard of. Joe knew his family was proud. But he'd avoided looking at them during his speech, and later, when he stood on the platform, his diploma in his hand, he could only think that at last he was on his own, with nothing further to keep him in Greenburg.

He hadn't said good-bye to his father; he had taken a bus one day while everyone was at work. Though his mother and Pete had taken him out for pizza and a movie the night before, his father had never even acknowledged his impending departure. The break had been made already. They had not spoken since the morning he'd refused to sign the forms. Now, working in Grantsport and living on his uncle's houseboat, Joe could think of himself as fatherless.

He wiped his hands on a rag and tried to find another station on the radio. Surely there must be one that didn't specialize in idiotic commentary. He'd be willing to settle for golden oldies. But everything else was static. He returned the dial to the rock station. It was just as well he couldn't afford a better radio, he reflected. At least if he listened to this stuff, he wouldn't have to explain to the other guys who worked for his uncle his preference for classical music or jazz.

He had only once been foolish enough to let anyone he'd grown up with know how he felt about classical music. Pete had driven him and some friends to Cincinnati one Saturday for an afternoon baseball game and he'd seen a poster for a concert in the park. He had suggested to the others that they might want to go there after the game. It was free after all, and the Cincinnati Symphony Orchestra was playing one of his favorites, Beethoven's "Eroica." It had taken him weeks to live down their reaction. He'd

40

never been to a live concert, and the disappointment of missing that chance was almost harder to handle than the taunts of the other guys. What little he knew about classical music he'd learned from the public radio station and the music teacher he'd had in junior high. College was to have given him the first opportunity he'd had to go to concerts, plays, opera. Greenburg had never offered him anything except books.

The local news was on, a more rational voice than that hyper disc jockey. Suddenly, Joe put down his wrench and listened. The newscaster was talking about Mayor Sterling. ". . . indicted today with Mayor Sterling was Charles W. Dyer, president of the local construction company that built the controversial and ill-fated gymnasium. At air time neither Mr. Dyer nor the mayor could be reached for comment."

Indicted? What for? But the newscaster had gone on to the forecast that the Ohio was bound to rise further before it began going down again, even if the rain did stop by the end of the day, as predicted. Joe thought about what he'd said to Amanda. He hadn't known, of course. Uncle Frank had treated it as if it had been a minor scandal, hardly worth repeating. It must have been much more serious if an indictment had been brought against the mayor. Had Amanda known? Had she come down to the marina to get away?

So much for Amanda Sterling. If he hadn't already known she was poison, this would clinch it. She'd never look at him now. What he'd said had been more hurtful than he could have guessed, far more than he'd intended. Despite his certainty that he would never have dared to show an interest in her, Joe was aware of a sense of great disappointment. It was as if a door had slammed in his face—a door he had slammed himself.

41

· 4 ·

As she drove, Amanda went over the last few minutes in her mind. Her hands still felt shaky, her grip on the wheel not quite certain. Despite the music blasting in her ears, she could still hear the mocking tone in his voice. Why had she been afraid of him? He hadn't threatened her. He'd done nothing at all except stand in the rain staring at her. Strange behavior maybe, but hardly terrifying. She had felt so alone out there on the dock, with the water behind her and Joe Schmidt in front of her and no one else anywhere around. Why had he said that about her father? It was hard to believe Frank Essig would tell anyone her father had been in any way responsible for what had happened.

Amanda wiped at the inside of the windshield with a Kleenex and turned on the defroster. Why didn't it stop raining? How crazy she was being, blaming everything on the rain. Joe Schmidt, after all, hadn't appeared because of the rain. He was just a guy. Not worth getting upset about. But she kept seeing him, the lanky toughness of him and that steady, insolent stare. His eyes were nothing special, just ordinary, dark brown eyes. There was no reason to think he could see anything more than anyone else. Except that it felt, when he had stared that way, as if he were seeing through her somehow, and that what he could see was unworthy, in need of hiding. It was as if the person

42

everyone knew as Amanda Sterling was a disguise she had put on to hide the person she really was, and that he was somehow able to see that real one. Obviously, that couldn't be true, and whatever was making her feel this way was coming from herself, not from him. He was just another mechanic from the marina. Infinitely forgettable. Except that she wasn't forgetting him. Except that she could still feel, in the hand that guided the steering wheel, the hard grip of his hand, and the sensation in her right shoulder of brushing against him as she had passed him on the dock.

She stopped at a traffic light and peered out at the rainy street corner. She must have been driving on automatic pilot. She had turned away from the river without being aware of it, and was nearly downtown. The cross street here was a state road. If she turned left she could go back out of town and just drive for a while. She remembered a roadside diner out that way where she could get something to eat. It was almost late enough to stop for lunch, and her stomach was reminding her insistently that she hadn't eaten breakfast. She turned down the radio a little. The sound had begun to give her a headache. Something had begun to give her a headache.

Amanda turned the dial, looking for the public radio station. If Steve wasn't going to ride in this car, she wasn't going to leave the radio on his favorite station, and that was that. When she had turned onto the state road and begun to drive away from town again, she found the station and recognized a Rachmaninoff piano concerto. She didn't like rock music very well. She preferred classical. As soon as she thought that, she realized that she wasn't sure it was true. Sometimes she liked rock, sometimes classical. It wasn't really possible to pick one and discard the other. She hated country. That was easy. But then it was easier for her to pin down the things she hated than to be clear on the things she liked. It didn't seem to be that way for anyone else. Actually, it hadn't always been that way for her, either. She used to like her friends, Steve, most things in her life. Until recently. Maybe that was why the rain was driving her so crazy. Maybe she needed to get out on the river again, needed to do the things she'd done every summer, to see if that, too, had changed. Would being on the river be enough, as it always had, or would she find herself still dissatisfied and confused?

The diner was just ahead, its parking lot uncrowded. Amanda would have it almost to herself at this hour, between breakfast and lunch. Good. She pulled the car into the parking lot and stopped under a dripping cottonwood tree. As she pulled on the emergency brake, the piano solo ended, and the announcer began the local news. She retrieved her purse from under the seat and froze, her hand on the ignition key, as she heard her father's name and the words that followed: "The collapse of the roof of Grantsport's controversial new gymnasium took over the headlines again today, after months of near silence, when the special grand jury returned two indictments. Grantsport's popular and charismatic mayor, James Sterling, was indicted on charges of taking kickbacks from the Dyer Construction Company in return for lending his support to their bid. Indicted with the mayor was Charles W. Dyer, president of the construction company. It is alleged that Mr. Dyer changed specifications for the materials used to build the clear-span roof, thus substantially lowering the cost of those materials. The changes apparently also resulted in the roof's inability to withstand the weight of the area's first major snowfall. The architectural firm that designed the building has maintained from the beginning of the investigation that the roof, as designed, should have stood up to far greater stress than that which caused the

44

collapse. Dyer has contested the architect's claim. He could not be reached for comment. Sterling has yet to meet with reporters, but an aide is quoted as saying that the mayor will make a statement when he has had a chance to review the details of the indictment. In other news . . ."

Amanda switched off the radio. The rain on the roof sounded like hail. It was impossible. The grand jury had gone wrong somewhere, had been lied to, or had misread the evidence. Something. Her father couldn't have accepted a kickback—a bribe. If Dyer had changed something, Dyer was the guilty one. What did an indictment mean—that there was enough evidence to warrant a trial, wasn't that it? It didn't mean that he was guilty. A trial would prove that he wasn't. She couldn't imagine her father as a defendant in a trial. He wasn't a criminal. There had to be a mistake.

There had been a lot of talk just after it happened, but her father had said that such accusations were inevitable. And the lawsuits. He'd said that people always jumped at the chance to sue somebody. But he'd also said that it would all die down, as it had seemed to do.

Her father had only gotten into it because of the fight that was threatening to do real damage to the fabric of the city's government. There had been all those factions fighting about whether the project should be undertaken at all. There had been the memorial foundation that had begun the project, the faction that wanted the money spent on a city building rather than a gymnasium, the faction that insisted such an expenditure on athletics was wrong when the school system itself was in financial trouble. James Sterling had stayed out of the battle until it had grown so divisive that city council members couldn't agree on any other subject either. Then he'd pointed out that by building the gymnasium, with its unique architectural features, the city would gain a contemporary landmark, and that by giving the job to a local construction company rather than accepting an out-of-town bid, the jobs would stay in Grantsport and help the overall economy. It hadn't seemed a huge point, but it had been enough to calm the waters.

The gym had been connected with her father after that principally because he went to great trouble to make the opening ceremony a major event, with a visit from the governor and a cluster of state and federal legislators. By the time the first game had been played in the new gym, it had begun to be known as Sterling's gym, despite its being named for the man whose foundation had financed it. By then, the divisions had seemed virtually forgotten.

Until that night in January when, in a few hours, the old wounds had been opened again. It had been an ordinary winter night, she remembered. There had been a basketball game, and the Warriors had won. She and Steve had come home sooner than they might have because it had started to snow pretty heavily just after nine, and they had decided to skip the celebration party. Her parents had been home when they arrived, playing backgammon in front of a roaring fire. So Steve had stayed and they'd made popcorn and played a round-robin backgammon tournament until the eleven o'clock news. Even then, the weather forecast had been for "moderate" snowfall and gradually falling temperatures. Steve had gone home; she had watched a late movie and then gone to bed.

When the telephone wakened her, she lay in bed for a while, wondering what could be important enough to warrant a call at that hour. Her clock radio, glowing greenly, announced that it was 4:25 A.M. She could hear her father's voice between silences, and finally got up, put on her robe, and went to look out the windows. One look, and she knew the call had to do with the snow. It was coming down so heavily that it seemed to pile higher on the porch roof as she watched. Wind swept around the turret of the old house and pushed the snow in great, eddying swirls. They'd have to have the trucks out already, if people were to get around in the morning. And even so, the way it was coming down, the streets would probably fill up faster than they could be cleared.

Her father and mother were talking then, but she couldn't make out what they were saying. She was about to go back to bed when light spilled out onto the porch roof, turning the falling snow to a glittering curtain. Her parents were moving around now. She heard a door slam. Was her father getting dressed? At this hour? Where could he be going? She went out into the hall and found Doug already there, blinking in the light he had just turned on. "Are they going to close the whole town or what?" he asked. "Obviously, there won't be school!"

"It's Saturday," Amanda reminded him.

"Rats!" he said. "What a waste of a perfectly good blizzard!"

Her father came into the hall, tucking in his shirt with a tie hanging loose around his neck. His mayor's uniform, Amanda noted, as Peg Sterling came out of the bedroom, holding his suit jacket. Looking at their faces, Amanda knew it was something bad. "The gym roof has collapsed," her father said, and went into the bathroom, slamming the door shut behind him.

"The new gym?" Doug asked. As if it could be any other. The old one had been torn down.

Peg Sterling only nodded and leaned against the wall, holding the jacket and staring into space.

"Is this what it means when they say the roof has fallen in?" Doug asked, his eyes twinkling.

"It isn't a joking matter."

47

"Sorry."

"Was it the snow?" Amanda asked.

"Apparently. They don't know anything yet except that there's nothing left but the walls and a pile of rubble."

"It's a good thing the snow didn't start sooner," Doug observed. "Or the roof might have fallen in during the basketball game."

"Oh, God!" their mother said and closed her eyes. "All those people."

"Including Steve and me," Amanda said. "I guess we're lucky."

"I doubt if many people will see it that way." James Sterling came out of the bathroom and took his jacket.

"Has anyone called Dyer?" his wife asked.

"He's in the Bahamas," he answered. "Won't that look great! Go back to bed, kids. There's nothing you can do."

"Sure there is," Doug said. "I'll get dressed and help you shovel. If you're going out there, you'll have a heck of a time getting the car down the drive. I'll sleep later."

Amanda offered to help too, but they had only two shovels, so she and her mother went to the kitchen and made coffee and cocoa. Her father came in only long enough to get the thermos they had filled for him and left. The others ate breakfast, listening for news on the radio. At six, the major news was the snow, but it wasn't until seven that the roof collapse was mentioned. Then the focus of the announcement was that no one had been in the building at the time, so no one had been hurt. The announcement took only a few seconds.

By the evening news, the emphasis had changed. By then, the point was made that whatever defects had brought the roof down could have brought it down at any time, killing basketball players and their fans. For a time, then, people had seemed to lose track of the fact that no one

48

had been hurt, and acted as if the imagined loss of lives had actually occurred. Letters to the editor of the paper had been plentiful and angry. Suddenly, James Sterling's connection with the gym was a major liability. At school, for a while, people treated Amanda as if her father had himself endangered all their lives. But eventually, people seemed to decide that the mayor, at least, had been acting in good faith in recommending Dyer. The investigation was aimed primarily at the construction company and the architectural firm that had designed the building. Or so Amanda had thought.

So it was going to start all over again, Amanda said to herself, sitting there in the parking lot, listening to the rain on the roof of the car. Or had it ever really stopped? Her friends had gone back to normal, the furor had died down. But she wondered now if the gym roof hadn't collapsed on her after all, shattering her security. If people could turn on her father, who or what was safe? Joe Schmidt must have known about the indictment. She rubbed at the back of her neck. This time, it would be worse. This time there was a charge of bribery and an indictment to give it a solid foundation. A trial would prove her father's innocence, of course. But in the meantime. . .

She wondered if her mother had known this was coming. Surely not. Surely she wouldn't have gone off to speak at a luncheon if she'd expected this. Amanda decided to go home. She would pick up Doug first; she wanted him to find out from her. Then, when their mother came home, they'd be there. Whatever was wrong between them, they would have to stick together now.

Doug, wearing safety goggles under his rain hat, was halfway up the cliff at the side of the road, balanced precariously, chipping away at a piece of rock with his geolo-

49

gist's hammer. Amanda pulled off the road beneath him and rolled down her window. The rain had slowed to a light but steady drizzle. "Come down!" she called.

"In a second. I've almost got it." He went on working with his hammer for a moment, slipped a bit of rock into his pocket, then clambered down to the weeds at the base of the cliff. He opened the passenger door. "What's up? I haven't even stopped for lunch yet."

"Get your stuff," Amanda said. "I want to talk."

"So talk. Afterwards, I'll get back to work."

"I said, get your stuff. Afterwards, we're going home."

Doug wiped his wet face with the back of his hand, leaving a streak of mud across his nose, and peered at her. "Is this as serious as you look?"

"Yes."

He went to an outcropping of rock, fished his canvas bag out from under it and carefully put away his goggles and hammer. Amanda rolled up her window, trying to decide how to phrase the news. There didn't seem to be any way except the most direct. He climbed in, shut the door, and looked at her expectantly, his face grave. "Well? How bad is it?"

"Dad's been indicted."

"Indicted?" He narrowed his eyes. "This is a joke, right? The rain has gone to your head."

"It's no joke. I just heard it on the radio. Dad was indicted by a special grand jury today. Mr. Dyer, too."

"About the gym? He didn't have anything to do with that."

"They say he took a bribe from Dyer and that's why he helped Dyer get the job."

"The world has gone mad." He took off his yellow rain hat and shook his head. "That's the craziest thing I've ever heard."

50

Amanda explained the charges as the announcer had.

"Well, if Dyer did what they say, something ought to be done about him. But Dad wouldn't have known he was going to do it, or he never would have gotten into it."

"They say he took money, Doug. That would be wrong whether he knew what Dyer was going to do or not. In fact, that would be wrong if Dyer hadn't done anything at all."

"Okay. But since Dad wouldn't take a bribe, there's no sweat."

Amanda shook her head. "Don't you remember how it was last winter, when there wasn't even any story about a bribe? Mayors don't get indicted every day. I have the feeling this is going to be big. And rotten."

"There will have to be a trial, won't there?" Doug asked, then went on without waiting for an answer. "You have to be proven guilty, and since Dad can't be guilty, they won't be able to prove anything, and they'll acquit him, and that's all it'll be."

Amanda wished she thought it would be as simple as that. Maybe all ten year olds had that kind of faith in the system, or maybe it was Doug's natural optimism. She knew that sometimes innocent people were found guilty. Or sometimes just the publicity of a trial could do as much damage as a guilty verdict, even if the defendant were finally acquitted. Especially a politician. So much depended on how people saw a man. The newscaster had called her father popular and charismatic. He was. But even though that helped him, he had complained about it often enough. The campaign posters that called him the "Sterling Candidate" and "A Man of Sterling Character" had been good strategy, but he had never liked them. He hated the superficial approach people took to politics. In the last election his opponent had been short, bald, and ordinary looking, and her father had said that it probably wouldn't

51

matter if the man had a record of good works a mile long—up against the "Sterling Candidate" he didn't have a chance.

So if her father had been elected because of his looks or his name, because of an image, anything that wrecked that image in people's minds could be the end of his career. And how seriously would the party take a man who'd been indicted when it came to choosing a candidate for governor?

"Let's go home," Doug said. "Does Mom know yet?"

"I don't know."

"I hope not. Or if she does, I hope the Junior League doesn't. Wouldn't that make her luncheon fun?"

"You have a weird sense of fun."

"True."

When they came through the back door, the phone was ringing. "Let it go," Doug advised. "Whatever it is, it probably won't be good."

But Amanda could never let a phone ring. She was always sure that it would be something very bad and important or very good and important, and disaster would strike if she didn't answer it. So she did, and was relieved to hear Steve's voice.

"Have you heard?"

"I've heard."

"Where have you been? I've been trying to get you for an hour!"

"Out. What did you want?"

"What do you mean, what did I want? Amanda, this is Steve! I've been worried about you."

Amanda sighed. Doug, having hung up his rain gear and taken off his muddy boots, came into the kitchen and mouthed, "Who?"

"I'm sorry, Steve," she said, and Doug nodded, then

opened the refrigerator door and disappeared behind it. "I'm upset. Don't take it personally."

"You want me to come over? You want to come over here?"

"No. Doug and I want to wait here till Mom comes home. Listen, Steve, we'll be okay. It's going to take a while to figure out what's happening, that's all. I'll call you later."

"Okay." Steve's voice registered his disappointment. All he wanted to do was to offer comfort, and she had hurt his feelings. But she didn't have the energy to deal with his feelings now. "But *do* call me. I mean it!"

"I will. Good-bye. And thanks, Steve."

"Yeah."

Amanda hung up and toed off her wet shoes. She'd left footprints all the way from the back door to the phone. At least cleaning them up would give her something to do. Now that they were home, there didn't seem to be any real point in being here.

Doug came out from behind the refrigerator door with a bowl of strawberries in one hand and a carton of milk in the other, and nudged the door shut with a bare foot. "In the face of a crisis, the only reasonable thing to do is eat. You want one of my sandwiches? They're peanut butter and marshmallow goop."

"Fluffer nutters? For lunch? No thanks."

"Don't be a bigot. They're nutritious—peanut butter for protein, with the milk to make it complete, and marshmallow for quick energy. They aren't much different from peanut butter and jelly. Anyway, you ought to eat something. You're getting one of your headaches."

"How can you tell?"

"Go look in a mirror sometime. You get little lines between your eyes." He pulled a brown paper sack out of his

53

fossil-collecting bag and extracted a slightly squashed sand-wich. "I read somewhere that when you hurt, you tense up against the pain and the tension makes the pain worse. If you didn't fight the headaches, maybe they wouldn't get so bad."

"Thanks, Doctor Sterling."

"Meantime, have some strawberries, lie down, and call me in the morning."

"Will you clean up the floor for me?"

"Why should I deprive you of the chance to be useful? The mess'll be here when you get up. I've got to classify the new specimens, now that you've dragged me away from the best site I've found all year."

"Sorry." Amanda hung her raincoat in the back hall and tossed her wet shoes down the basement steps. "I don't know why I thought we should come home."

"It's the herding instinct. Or maybe the wagon train syndrome. You know, get the wagons in a circle and face outward to the enemy. I don't mind, Mandy. I'd rather be home, too. I am part of this wagon train, after all."

Amanda took a few strawberries and went to her room. Maybe it wasn't the herding instinct or the wagon train syndrome, she thought. Maybe it was just a need to be home. Like heading for shore when a storm was coming. Her room, with its turret windows, its twin beds, whose quilts matched the window seat cover, the stuffed animals she'd collected over the years, the desk her grandfather had made, felt safe. It was the same as ever, no matter what changed outside. Here, James Sterling could be just Dad, the man who woke her up on school mornings, and even at her age, kissed her good night before he went to bed him-self. She sat on her bed and ate her strawberries, then slid down and put her throbbing head on her pillow. She

54

wouldn't be able to sleep, but maybe Doug was right. If she could just lie there for a while and relax, maybe the headache would get better. Moments later, Amanda was asleep.

·5·

Amanda awoke to the sound of the back door slamming, and her mother's voice. "Douglas? Amanda? Are you here?"

Doug called down from his room, and Amanda sat up, rubbing her eyes. She could hardly believe the clock. Could she possibly have slept until two thirty? She sat on the edge of the bed for a moment, trying to get her bearings. A sense of menace hung over her. She must have been dreaming. That was it. She had been dreaming that a man, a man she didn't recognize but felt that she should know, had been threatening her with some kind of weapon. Whatever the weapon had been, it hadn't been threatening enough to terrify her, to make the dream a true nightmare, but it had made her very nervous. She hadn't known whether to run or to stand up to him. She could remember thinking that her usual response to everything was to run, and wondering why she wasn't doing that this time. It was as if she'd been caught by the man's eyes, pierced by them, but drawn to them, too. And all the time that maddening sense of being reminded of something, or of someone, and that vague menace.

"Come on, Mandy." Doug stuck his head around her door. "Let's get the wagons in a circle!"

Amanda followed Doug down the stairs, trying to shake the memory of the dream, trying to defog her brain. Now that her mother was home, what were they going to do? Or say to each other? The idea of circling the wagons, of sticking together, seemed right. But what did that really mean? Could Amanda and Peg Sterling suddenly pull together and help each other? Well, they could try. Maybe the thing to do was to watch Doug. He always seemed to do or say the right thing.

Peg Sterling was pacing between the sink and the kitchen table like a caged tiger, her heels clicking out a steady tattoo on the still-muddy white floor. She had thrown her suit jacket over the back of a chair and her green blouse emphasized the green of her eyes, which snapped with a kind of vibrant electricity. "Have you two heard the news?"

"That's why we came home," Doug said. "Mandy heard it on the radio."

"I'm sorry you had to find out that way."

"Is there a good way?" Amanda asked.

Her mother narrowed her eyes at her for a moment. "I assume that was not meant to be sarcastic."

"Did you know this morning?" Doug asked.

"I didn't know a thing until Dick Wolfe appeared at the Junior League luncheon and took me out into the hall to explain."

"Before or after your speech?"

"Before." She rubbed at her forehead. "It was a lovely lead-in! It was all I could do to get up and open my mouth."

"What did you say?"

"Exactly what I'd planned to say. No one there had heard the news yet, after all. Since it would be the last chance I'd have to say anything before the story was out, I decided to go ahead the way I'd planned. Except that I managed to sneak in a few of my old standard reminders about what your father has done for Grantsport."

"Have you talked to Dad?" Amanda asked.

"Not yet. He hasn't talked to the press yet, either. Dick says they're still going over the details themselves." The phone rang, and Amanda thought it sounded about ten times louder than usual. Her mother picked up the receiver. "Hello? . . . Yes, this is Peg Sterling. . . . Yes, of course I've heard the charges, and they're absurd. . . . I'm afraid I haven't anything else to say at this time." And she hung up. "Here we go again."

"Why don't we take the phone off the hook?" Amanda suggested.

"No. I want your father to be able to reach me if he wants to. I can handle the press by now." She resumed her pacing. "I'll bet Drew Norton is behind this somehow, the bastard!"

Doug raised his eyebrows at Amanda. Peg Sterling didn't use such language, especially in front of her children.

"Ever since the election, ever since his challenge to the vote count was thrown out of court, he's been after your father. He never took a stand on the gym at all until he knew where your father stood. Then he got into it on the side of those idiots who were trying to get the memorial committee to build an office building or something. Anything to work against your father's endorsement of the project. Norton must have some help with this one, though. He must have some connections with the grand jury. Has the phone been ringing a lot?" She looked at Amanda. "I see you answered it at least once."

Amanda looked at her footprints on the floor. Didn't her mother miss anything? "Just that once. I'll clean up the floor later. Steve called."

Peg Sterling stopped pacing and smiled. "The Randolphs are fine people, Amanda. And good friends. I'm glad Steve

58

called, because over the next few weeks you'll be glad to have him around. Did he ask you over?"

"Yes, but I thought I should be here when you came home."

"You don't have to stay home because of me. Go ahead and go over."

"Well—I . . ." Amanda didn't know what else to say. You didn't get family solidarity just by wanting it. But she didn't want to see Steve just now.

Doug came to her rescue. "She can't, Mom. When you circle the wagons, nobody's allowed to leave until we're sure who the enemy is and how strong."

"All right," Peg Sterling said. But Amanda wasn't fooled. It was only a temporary acquiescence to Doug—because he was Doug. Her mother began filling the coffeepot with water. "If the wagons are circling, I'm going to have coffee. But we know who the enemy is, Doug. And I doubt that he's very strong. We'll just have to see what kinds of weapons he has."

Amanda was reminded of her dream. Had it been about the indictment? Had the threat been to her father? It hadn't seemed to be. But with dreams, it was hard to tell. Everyone had a way of changing identities. It was hard to remember clearly anyhow.

"I'm going up to finish putting away the new specimens," Doug said. "I got sidetracked while I was looking one up and ended up reading all afternoon. But I'll be back in a few minutes."

When Doug had left, and Peg Sterling had finished grinding the coffee and putting it into the drip basket, she turned back to her daughter. "Listen to me, Amanda. Steve's loyalty isn't important just because you may feel the need of friends while this mess lasts. We have to be

59

very careful about how we react to the indictment. If we seem too threatened by it, people will think it's true. That's one reason I went ahead and gave the speech I'd planned to give today instead of excusing myself. I don't want to let anyone think we're in a panic. We have to rise above it. If people see that we can dismiss it as unimportant or just a temporary nuisance, they'll be able to dismiss it, too. So I want you to do your best to go on with your life in a normal fashion."

"Okay."

Her mother narrowed her eyes again. It was an expression Amanda was aware of more and more often. As if her mother were assessing her dependability, gauging how far she could be trusted. Or if she could be trusted at all. "I don't mean normal as in the last couple of weeks. I mean normal for a summer vacation. I mean that I want you to start seeing Steve again and quit moping around the house the way you've been doing. If it means playing pinball, then play pinball. If it means going to a movie, go to a movie. Until you can get back out on the river, you're going to have to do whatever it is everyone else is doing."

Amanda looked out the window. The trees were still dripping in the backyard, but the rain had stopped. "Don't give me that sullen face. This is not between you and me now, Amanda. This is not me trying to get you to do something you don't want to do. So don't react the way you always do to that. We haven't time for this tiresome adolescent–parent conflict right now. This is for your father—for the whole family. And it is very, very important. We've got to make it clear to all of Grantsport that this indictment is a farce and that we are not going to let it change anything. Do you understand what I'm saying?"

Amanda nodded. She understood. She would do it if she

had to. It wasn't as if she hated Steve or anything. But her stomach seemed to clench into a hard knot. This *was* for her father, of course. But how conveniently it fit with what her mother had been trying to force on her anyway. The way things were, she couldn't fight back.

Doug came back into the kitchen and her mother announced that she was going to make a double batch of chocolate chip cookies. Doug offered to help. He'd been known to eat half a batch of chocolate chips even before the dough was out of the mixing bowl.

Amanda leaned back in her chair and watched her mother take an apron from the drawer and tie it on, then carefully roll up the sleeves of the silk blouse. Some people, Amanda thought, would at least kick off the high heels. Or even change clothes entirely. Peg Sterling was the only person she could imagine starting to bake cookies dressed like that, apron or no apron. Amanda tried to remember how she had felt about her mother when she was very little, when Doug was a baby and she had been the one offering to help make the cookies. There had been something warm and comforting about working in the kitchen with her mother then. A sense of dependence that had felt good. And when she'd glance up at her mother, there had always been a kind of awe at her beauty. She had wanted more than anything to grow up to be just like her. She had dreamed of herself in an apron in her own kitchen, baking cookies or cakes or bread. Or dressing up to go out to some terribly important meeting. She had believed then that when her mother had gone out to a meeting, it had always been important, some mysterious adult activity that kept the world going. That was before she'd found out what the Junior League and the DAR and the rest of them were like. Back then, Amanda had not noticed how much time her mother spent maintaining that awesome beauty, put-

61

ting on makeup, choosing her wardrobe, having her hair done. She couldn't remember when everything had changed, but the vision of the perfect mother wouldn't come again, no matter how she tried to get it back. There were too many cracks in it now.

The attention Amanda had received all her life, the fussing to be sure that she had just the right dress and just the right hairdo, had for a very long time seemed to be proof of her mother's love. With a child's assumption that she was the center of the universe, Amanda had believed that everything her mother had done for her had been exactly that—for her. Done out of love. But eventually, she'd noticed that her mother fussed over Doug in exactly the same way. And most of it had to do with how they looked or what people would think of them.

Then Amanda had noticed the way her mother would look around her in a crowd, her eyes shrewd and judgmental, until someone looked back. Then would come the smile. Instantly. Turned on the way you turned on a light. And turned off just as quickly. Amanda had begun to have trouble distinguishing her mother the public person from her mother at home—this mother who at home almost never wore slacks and never jeans, who baked bread and made casseroles to take to potluck suppers. When the newspaper articles would appear extolling the mayor's wife who baked her own bread and invented wonderful new casseroles without ever neglecting her civic responsibilities, Amanda had wondered whether the articles were written because of what her mother happened to be like, or whether her mother was like that so that the articles could be written.

There had never been any trouble, on the other hand, telling the mayor of Grantsport from the man who was her father. There were similarities, of course, between the man who stood with his family to have his picture taken and the man who still kissed her good night. But she could tell the difference. In public, her father would put an arm around his wife and the other around her or Doug, and there would be a picture for the public of the caring between them. But at home there was so much more. At home there were the sparkling blue eyes and the jokes. James Sterling the mayor gave a good speech and could make people laugh when he wanted them to, but James Sterling the father made some of his best jokes at the expense of the mayor. He always seemed to know the difference between his image and himself. Amanda wondered if there were any difference for her mother. She'd seen a pantomime once about a person who put on a mask and then couldn't get it off again, as if his face had grown to fit it. That was Peg Sterling. There must have been a woman, once, who put on the role of political wife. Now there was just the political wife.

"Hey, Mandy, are you going to help with these or not?" Doug asked, as he dragged the flour canister out of a lower cupboard.

"No thanks."

"Remember the Little Red Hen," he warned. "Who doesn't help bake the bread doesn't get to help eat it."

"Even you couldn't eat every cookie in a double batch. I'll take my chances."

"Besides," Peg Sterling said. "It's almost impossible for all three of us to work on the same project. She can do the floor afterwards."

"All right, but it doesn't seem fair."

The phone rang. "I'll be phone answerer," Amanda said. "Okay?"

Her mother, in the process of measuring the margarine, nodded. "If it's a reporter, just say you don't know anything about it."

It was a reporter. "You want to speak to Mrs. Sterling?" she repeated, looking to her mother for a response. Her mother shook her head. "I'm sorry, she can't come to the phone at the moment. This is Amanda Sterling. Can I help you?" When the reporter asked what she thought of her father's indictment, she bit her lip. She wanted to tell him what she thought of it. "I'm sorry, I don't know what you're talking about. Good-bye." She hung up. "I don't like this," she said. "Can't we just leave it off the hook?"

"Not until your father gets home. Besides, friends may call, too, and I need to know they're out there."

"Okay. But I take back my offer. I'm no good at dealing with reporters."

"I'll get it from now on," Peg Sterling said. "I'm used to it."

"I could answer and say it was the Museum of Zoological History. That ought to throw them," Doug said, as he cracked an egg into the mixing bowl. "Or maybe Doug's Cookie Factory. How would that be?"

"I'll take care of it, thanks just the same."

So Amanda went back up to her room and sat at her window, watching the river. The phone rang more and more often. Clearly, the word was getting around. After the evening news, it could only get worse. Eventually, the smell of the cookies reached her, and she remembered that she'd eaten nothing but a few strawberries all day. Lured by the aroma, she went back down and found Doug and her mother at the kitchen table, playing gin rummy and eating cookies. Peg Sterling's face look strained; the lines around her eyes that were normally almost invisible under her makeup were marked out like small roads on a map.

"Who's winning?" she asked, taking a still-warm cookie from the cooling racks on the counter.

"Who do you think?" her mother said.

Doug grinned. "She isn't concentrating. You should hear some of the phone calls!"

Peg Sterling slapped a card upside down on the discard pile. "Gin. Ha! Pride goeth before a fall, young man!"

"What are the calls like?" Amanda asked.

"I hardly wait to find out anymore. Cranks, mostly. June Randolph called, though, and Julie's mother. So far the baddies are in the lead."

"I answered one," Doug said, looking up from the figures on the score pad. "Some lady wanted to know how I liked having a near-murderer for a father. I said it was okay, but that I hoped next time he'd really get somebody."

"That was his last call!" their mother said. "How am I doing now?" she asked him.

"Your gin wasn't enough. You're still forty-three points behind." The phone rang again and Peg Sterling groaned.

"I'll get this one," Amanda said. "We're in this together, after all." But she didn't have a chance to see how she'd deal with a crank. It was Steve again.

"Julie's having a party tonight," he said. "She thought we should all get together and let you know we're on your side. You will go with me, won't you?"

Amanda was surprised to find that she wanted to go. Not because of her mother's request. Not even because it was supposed to be good for her father to behave "normally." She wanted to get away. "Sure, I'll go."

"I'll pick you up about eight."

"Okay. See you then."

"Going out?" Peg Sterling asked when she hung up.

"He's picking me up around eight. Julie's having a party."

"I'm glad you're going."

Amanda decided to let her mother think she was going for her sake. As Doug began to shuffle the cards, they heard the front door open. "Where's the Sterling family?" her father's voice called. "And what is that super smell?"

They looked at each other, and at the clock. Only four fifteen. "Out here," Doug yelled. "And chocolate chip cookies. What are you doing home so early?"

James Sterling came into the kitchen, his jacket over one shoulder, his tie loosened. "I need a kiss from my wife, a hug from my kids, a cookie, and a good, stiff drink. More or less in that order."

Peg Sterling went to him, put her arms around him and kissed him. They stood for a moment, looking at each other as if they were able to take something from each other, or give it, with their eyes alone. Doug handed his father a cookie, and the embrace was broken. "Mmmm, terrific!" He pulled Doug in to share the hug, and Amanda joined them. "I want you all to know that one of the things that kept me going today was knowing I would eventually get away and come home to you."

"See? It *is* the herding instinct," Doug said.

"You may be right." James Sterling sat down on the kitchen stool, one foot resting on the step. "The reason I'm home so soon is because Dick Wolfe saw a chance to get me out of city hall without having to bore my way through a wall of reporters. They had somebody watching my car so I couldn't make a getaway, so he brought around his wife's car. I sent someone out the front to tell them about a press conference . . ."

"Today?" Amanda asked.

"No, but they didn't know that at the time. They were all clustered around the front except the guy who was watching the car, so Dick and I ducked out a side door into

66

his wife's Chevette and here I am. We've got a little time before they catch on to the fact that I've left."

"Time?" Doug asked. "For what?"

"Time before they come here."

Peg Sterling nodded, but Amanda and Doug were surprised. "You mean reporters will come here to the house?"

Their father took a sip of the gin and tonic his wife had just handed him and nodded. The phone rang and Doug started toward it. "Take it off the hook," James Sterling said. "That's why they'll come here. They know how easy it is to hang up on someone, or just to leave the phone off the hook. They want to ask questions and for that they have to come where I am. I'm afraid when they discover I'm not downtown anymore, it won't be any time at all before they'll show up here. It's going to be a little hard for a while to find any privacy. Reporters can be devilishly persistent."

"Sorry, you must have the wrong number," Doug was saying. "This is Wo Fing's Egg Roll Stand and Taco Shop." He hung up the phone, waited a moment, and then put the receiver into a drawer and closed the drawer on the cord. "That'll take care of them!"

"And taco shop?"

"Sure. You wouldn't want your son to be an ethnic bigot, would you?"

James Sterling smiled, but for once the smile looked like one of his wife's, Amanda thought. It didn't reach his eyes at all. His always rugged face seemed even more deeply lined and rugged than usual, and pale. Too pale.

"Sit down, kids. I want to talk to your mother for a bit, but first I want to explain some things." They sat. Their mother began putting the cookies into a plastic container. "I am, for the moment, a media event. Reporters and cameramen are going to be swarming all over me."

67

"Are we going to have to sneak out of the house the way you sneaked out of the office today?" Doug asked.

"We couldn't, even if we tried. But you'll have to be prepared for the way things will be. These guys will do their best to interview you. Both of you. They'll try to get you to say something they can use against me. It depends on which side they're on, of course, but I suspect they'll mostly be after the negative."

"I thought journalists were supposed to be objective," Doug said.

"And leprechauns give away pots of gold."

"But why would they try to get us to say anything they can use against you? The press have always been pretty good to you, I thought," Amanda said.

"That's true." He held out his glass, which his wife took to refill. "But this story is a big one. A mayor indicted. For a while, just the indictment will be story enough. But pretty soon they'll have to have something else to say. There won't be a trial for a long time yet. In the meantime, every reporter in southern Ohio is going to decide he has a mission to track down the 'truth.' For most of them that will mean proving the charges of the indictment before the case ever goes to trial."

"They want you to be guilty?" Doug asked.

"Of course. If I'm not, where's their story? If the roof collapsed purely by accident and no one was hurt, the building will be rebuilt, and that will be that. But if somebody can be blamed for it, that'll make up to the reporters for the fact that it didn't come down on hundreds of fans in the middle of a basketball game."

Amanda shuddered. "You mean they'd have preferred that people had been killed?"

"If you asked a reporter, he'd deny it. But in general,

yes, because it makes a bigger story. If a tornado touches down or a volcano erupts, if there's an earthquake or a flood, any of those stories would have great possibilities. But if no one is hurt and there's no major damage, the story is over quickly and forgotten. There's no one to blame and nothing to keep the story alive. If there are grieving families to interview, or mass funerals to attend, pictures to be taken of houses torn off their foundations, speculations to be made about what might have happened to the people who are missing—that kind of story can go on for days, even weeks."

"That's disgusting."

"The human race is ghoulish," Doug said.

"Anyway, the point here is that these people will try to talk to you. There will be cameramen around the house, and people ringing the doorbell. Wherever you go, a reporter could turn up and start asking questions. So I want you to understand that you aren't to talk to anyone. None of your cute tricks, either, Doug. Even you could get tripped up talking to a reporter. Whatever they ask you, *whatever*, you just say 'no comment.' That's all. Understand?"

"But what if they say things that aren't true? If I just say 'no comment,' won't it look as if I think what they're saying is true?"

"Amanda, there is no way to win with these guys. No matter what you say, they'll find some way to make it mean what they want it to mean. They can do that to some extent with 'no comment,' too, but people get bored with that very fast. In the long run, it's the safest thing."

Amanda frowned. She thought of all the times she'd seen people on the television news pushing their way through crowds of reporters murmuring "no comment" all the way through. She'd always assumed they were guilty when they did that. It made them look guilty. "I don't like it."

Her mother's voice was sharp. "You don't have to like it. You just have to do it."

Her father put his hand over hers. His hand was cold and damp from holding his glass, but even so it was comforting. "It won't be easy. Someone is bound to say something you'd like to argue about. But there's no percentage in arguing with them. No matter what they say."

"Okay," Amanda agreed reluctantly. What else could she do?

"And another thing. There's no point reading all about this in the papers, or listening to the local news. What they report may be untrue, or at the very least, distorted. There's no sense getting worked up about it. There are plenty of things to do about this, none of them public. Count on it that I'll be doing those things, and that we're going to come out of it just fine. What the media will say and what is really going on are likely to be very different things."

"What about libel laws?" Doug protested. "And slander! People can't just tell lies, can they? Isn't there something you can do about that?"

"It would be better to ignore it for the time being. What we have to do right now is to let it blow over. Think of it as a storm. There's a big wind and lots of thunder and lightning. It feels very dangerous. But it will pass. In fact, the more ferocious it is, the faster it's likely to be gone. We just have to batten down the hatches and wait it out."

"In a safe harbor," Peg Sterling said. "That's what this house is. A safe harbor."

It sounded too pat, Amanda thought. Her mother was acting again. And anyway, if a storm was bad enough,

70

there wasn't any such thing as a safe harbor. Storms could do real damage. Terminal damage. Her father wasn't admitting that, but she was almost sure he was thinking it, underneath the confidence. She wished the trial would be immediate. The sooner the truth could get out, the better.

·6·

Joe sat on his bunk in the middle cabin of his uncle's houseboat, a pillow propped behind him. He had a legal pad on his knee and a ball point in his hand, but aside from the words "character sketch" at the top of the page, he hadn't written anything. He was staring, instead, at the paneling of the cabin walls.

Before dinner, when he'd finished work and was about to come back to the houseboat, Chick and Jim, the other two mechanics, had asked him to go out with them later. They had a couple of six-packs stashed in the back of Chick's car and they planned to cruise through town to see if they could drum up any action. If they were lucky, they said, they'd pick up some girls and go down to the park by the river. He'd been tempted for a moment. Not that he wanted to go with them. The prospect of an evening with girls they were likely to pick up on a night like this, girls who would be attracted to Pete's car, with its orange flames on the hood, its mag wheels and packed pipes, was anything but inviting. But it would be a chance to set his relationship with the other guys. He'd be working with them all summer, and tonight would have been a first step in convincing them he was one of them.

For some reason, he hadn't been ready for an evening like that—a night like that. From their description of the last such trip, he knew they'd been out until nearly four A.M., though they had both managed to get to work the next morning. Joe knew he could manage without sleep as well as the other two, but somehow the timing was wrong. He just didn't want to go out with them yet. So he'd made an excuse about having a job to do for his uncle, and then had let them know that he'd be up for it the next time they went out. He couldn't refuse to go along with them very often, not if he wanted them to accept him. Probably, he couldn't refuse them even once more except for a real and obvious reason. He smiled grimly to himself. It was like having to have a written excuse for missing school. The world was always putting obligations on you of one kind or another.

It wasn't that he didn't like Chick or Jim. They were okay. They knew their jobs and they did them. The fact that they could also drink most of the night and still show up for work the next day at least showed a sense of responsibility. It was the bigots of the world who thought a man had to be a doctor or a lawyer to be conscientious or dependable.

The trouble was, Joe didn't feel he belonged with them any more than he had ever belonged in his neighborhood, or in his own family for that matter. He felt fundamentally different. Joe didn't have a car, for one thing. It was only partly because he needed the money for other things. It was also because he didn't really care about having one. There was nothing he wanted to do that he couldn't manage to do without a car—for now at least. Or if he did need a car for something, there was almost always someone willing to lend him one. At home it was usually Pete; here it was Uncle Frank. For Chick, though, the black Camaro with the orange flames was perhaps the most important object in his life. Keeping up the payments on the car, keeping its gas tank full, is what made Chick so conscientious about his job. Jim said that Chick didn't need a girl friend because he cared more about his car than he could possibly care for a person. "If he can't screw his car," Jim had said, "at least it comes in handy when he finds someone he can!"

When Joe thought about girls, it wasn't that he never thought about them that way, only that he had something else in mind. He'd seen the direction that could lead all too often. He didn't want a pregnant teenage wife, a child to support, a divorce by the age of twenty-five. He'd rather wait, no matter how long it took. He had a very definite plan, and when he imagined himself with someone, he imagined a bright, educated career woman. They would be friends, companions, lovers, perhaps husband and wife. But they would be together for the rest of their lives, once they'd found each other. Because they would have a great deal in common and because they would have waited long enough to know what it was they were really looking for. That would all be later. Much later. After he had finished with school. Joe's plans were very clear in his mind, and they didn't jibe at all with Chick's, if Chick had any plans beyond his next car payment.

Chick and Jim weren't dumb, either. He wasn't an intellectual snob, Joe told himself. He knew the difference between school smart and what his father called life smart. Jim and Chick might fail history exams or be rotten at composing essays on Holden Caulfield's despair in *Catcher in the Rye*, but they probably knew the lyrics to every rock song for the last three years, could explain the most intricate football maneuver, and give the batting averages of every player in the National League, with emphasis on the Cincinnati Reds. They knew how to get a loan for a car, how to judge by the clouds and the color of the sky whether a storm was likely to pass over or might clobber the marina.

Most of those things were things Joe couldn't do, didn't know. Joe could get an A+ on the Holden Caulfield essay, could finish college calculus in high school, could talk about existential despair—so that is what he had done. There wasn't time for anyone to do everything, to learn everything. If he hadn't been born a Schmidt, he wouldn't know any more about engines, probably, than a surgeon who knew the intricacies of the human brain but whose Mercedes would be an eternal mystery. Joe had had to work at learning enough about sports to carry on conversations with the athletic types he had grown up with. But he could never understand their fascination with games he found mostly boring and repetitious.

He'd spent his life like a chameleon, trying to take on the color of his surroundings, learning to do things he didn't like. It wasn't only sports. He didn't like the taste of beer. That was something he had never admitted to anyone. Joe thought he'd probably drunk gallons of beer by the time he'd finished high school, and had never enjoyed a swallow of it, except on those rare occasions when he was so hot and the beer so cold that it had been at least refreshing. He'd only been drunk once. The experience had been so painful, so humiliating, that once he'd recovered enough to walk around and to think straight, he'd promised himself that he would never let it happen again. It was just one more of the things he couldn't understand about people around him. And it wasn't only the guys from his own class, the kids of the blue-collar workers, it was most of the guys he knew. They actually set out on purpose to get drunk. It was a form of recreation. They didn't seem to mind the feeling of being out of control. They didn't even mind being desperately ill, kneeling over toilet bowls, or vomiting out car windows. And then there was Joe's reverence for his own life. He didn't want to end it before he was twenty, smashed against a telephone pole or a bridge abutment on some country road in the state of Ohio. But that never seemed to bother the others. He wondered if they ever even considered their own mortality. Or did they think of themselves as invincible? Six-Million-Dollar Men who were such experts with cars, or here on the river, with boats—that they couldn't possibly have an accident, no matter how drunk they got? Or perhaps, Joe reflected, they just drank, and by the time they were drunk, could no longer tell how badly messed up they really were.

Joe stretched out his legs on his bunk, letting the legal pad slide off onto the floor. He wanted to be a writer. But how could he be when he couldn't get inside people who were different? How, he wondered, could he ever write a character like any of the guys he knew, when he couldn't understand what made them act the way they did? When he couldn't imagine how they felt. He'd lived among people who were different all his life, and still couldn't understand them. Even when he acted like them, he couldn't make it feel right. He supposed that he really wasn't very smart himself, no matter what his school grades or his SATs might say. Maybe his father was right.

It bothered him that it didn't bother anyone else, this not being able to understand. His father didn't mind at all not being able to understand Joe. He assumed that if Joe was different, then Joe was wrong, or weird. It never seemed to occur to his father that being able to understand his son was valuable in any way, unless it happened automatically, the way he understood Pete, his oldest. And then, he only assumed that Pete was okay while Joe was not.

Joe had read somewhere—he couldn't remember where—that all the major problems in history could be traced to people's tendency to think in terms of "we" and "they." All the wars, crusades, inquisitions, pogroms—all the agony—had been caused by the inability of one kind of person to understand another kind, to see inside other minds enough to find some common ground. "We are right," is what people thought. And "we" are different from "them." Therefore, they are wrong and we must either convince or destroy them. Since the same thoughts afflicted "them," people were always being destroyed.

Joe thought of himself as stuck between the "we's" and the "they's." It was as if he were an alien, unable to relate properly to any of the varieties of earthlings. Or at least any he'd encountered so far. He had thought, for a time, that he was more like the guys who came from a different social world, but who did well in school and even liked it. He had felt closer to them. But they hadn't returned the feeling. Outside of class, the way he dressed, the part of town he lived in, made him too different. And so he'd recognized at last that he was, for everyone, a "they." And he had no "we" at all. Only "I."

He had come here after dinner to do a character sketch of his aunt, a woman who held a great fascination for him. Aunt Myra went against every expectation he had had of her on first sight. Talk about different! He leaned over and picked up his pad again. Actually, he might have a better chance at writing about Aunt Myra decently than about someone like Chick or Jim. At least she was so very different that he could let his imagination go and find out where it led him. Maybe that is what a writer had to rely on, finally. Imagination. He hadn't known Aunt Myra very well when he'd come to Grantsport. The two families had visited back and forth a few times when he was little

77

and the Essig children had still been at home. But they had married and moved away. When there weren't any children to get together, the family visits had stopped. The Aunt Myra he remembered had been big—even fat; Joe supposed she had always been fat. But not as fat as she was now. Myra Essig was quite possibly the fattest person he had ever seen. Her eyes seemed almost lost in the round, soft face, her body was made up entirely of mounds and rolls of fat. His first reaction had been of distaste. He had assumed that eventually he would learn to find her appearance tolerable, but he'd been astonished to discover that he hardly ever noticed. Almost immediately, he had liked her. Very much. As everyone seemed to.

He'd expected her to eat a lot. How else did someone get to look like that? But he had thought she would hoard food. He'd thought that when she put food on the table, he would have to eat quickly to get his share. It was a little that way at home, where only his father had ever routinely gotten second helpings, and everyone else had had to take as much the first time around as he could get away with. But Aunt Myra wasn't like that at all. She was generous with food. Almost too generous. If he ate only two mettwursts and one helping of sauerkraut and mashed potatoes as he had tonight, she practically forced him to take more. She did the cooking at the coffee shop and she did it well. The food was good, but it was also plentiful. She said that people who'd been on the river or working on their boats always had a big appetite. She loved to see people enjoy the food she made for them. It was as if she were sharing the most important thing in her world with them—as if feeding people was her way of showing them how much she cared about them.

And she did care. For all sorts of people. Joe shook his head. Aunt Myra was the exception, he guessed. She thought of everybody as "we." Maybe she was so big that she felt like the world itself. She treated all the boys who worked for her husband as if they were her own sons. She treated the people who moored their boats at the marina as if they were family. She assumed that the wealthiest people were equal to her, and their response was to assume that she was equal to them. One big family. Even at his most cynical, Joe could not come up with a selfish reason for her being the way she was.

During dinner tonight, they had been talking about the evening news, about the indictment of the mayor, and when she talked about the family, he had seen the tears in her eyes. "What a dreadful thing it is for them," she'd said. "For Peg and the kids." And then she'd gone into a tirade about the villains in the city government. "They've been after Jim Sterling from the first," she said, looking to Uncle Frank for corroboration. Uncle Frank, ever taciturn, nodded. "He's just too good. I can't understand why people always seem to want to bring good people down." She took a bite of mashed potatoes, swallowed, and went on, gesturing with her fork. "Jim Sterling will come out of this all right. He's an honest man and a trial will prove it. Anyway, he's the best mayor this town's had. But just think how hard it's going to be on Peg. On all of them." She looked at Joe. "Amanda was here this morning. Did you see her? She's the one with that little white car."

"I saw her," Joe said. He was glad his aunt didn't know what he'd said to Amanda that morning.

"Pretty, isn't she?"

Not *pretty*, Joe thought, but the flutter in his chest was unmistakable.

"And you should meet that little brother of hers. That Doug. What a kid—smart as a whip." She grinned, her eyes almost disappearing behind her cheeks. "Could be

79

smarter than you, even! And only ten years old. Eats like a horse, that boy. He told me once that it takes a lot of food to run that brain of his. He's a joker too. Gets it from his dad." Her mood had changed then, the lines of her face all seemed to droop downward. "I hate to see them in trouble. Did Amanda seem depressed to you? Or didn't you get to see her that close?"

"She didn't seem depressed." At least not until I'd finished with her, he thought.

Joe left the table soon after. He was wishing the meeting with Amanda had never happened. Bad luck. Oh, well, if there had ever been someone different, a "they," it was Amanda Sterling.

Joe put his pen into his shirt pocket. This was ridiculous. Now that he'd worked himself around to thinking about Amanda Sterling, he wasn't likely to write much of a character sketch. The symptoms were clear. He glanced around the cabin. Aside from the bunk, it contained only a small dresser and an alcove with hangers. There was no good place to write except this way, on the bunk, and for some reason, this position didn't work. It was too relaxed. He couldn't keep his mind concentrated. And right now, all mental roads were likely to lead to Amanda Sterling, whether he liked it or not.

He stood up, then, and stretched. He was not about to make a fool of himself over Amanda Sterling. Any more than he had already. He picked up his fatigue jacket from the end of the bunk, put it on, and slipped his legal pad inside it, under his arm. In the forward cabin, Uncle Frank was stretched out on the hide-a-bed couch, watching a baseball game on television, and Aunt Myra was hidden behind the newspaper, grumbling quietly to herself about whatever she was reading.

"I'm going out for a while," Joe said. "Mind if I take the lantern?"

His uncle nodded without taking his eyes from the game. Aunt Myra lowered the paper and looked at him. "Is it raining?"

"Not anymore."

"You want a snack to take along? How long will you be gone?"

"I don't need anything. I just thought I'd go for a walk, now that the rain has stopped. I think I'll go down by the river."

"Watch out for the mud! You could lose a leg to it in some places."

"That's okay," Joe grinned. "I've got another one." She went back to her paper, and Joe took the battery-operated lantern out onto the front deck. He could stay there and work on the white metal table, but he wasn't ready to let his aunt and uncle know about his writing. Not until he knew them better and could be sure they wouldn't treat it the way his father had.

He stepped onto the dock, the lantern light throwing a grayish circle around him in the mist. Where to go? Where could he find a place to sit, in the dark, to write? Maybe a wet tree stump beside the Ohio River amongst the mosquitoes and the poison ivy. That ought to be enough to prove his determination. If nothing else, it might give him a story someday. Joe chuckled as he walked up the gangway. He was beginning to feel like Dracula, as if he had a terrible secret. He had to go out at night to satisfy his bloodlust.

A path had been made along Ryan Creek by local fishermen who regularly fished the point where it emptied into the river. He started along that path, his light glinting off puddles where the ground dipped. He managed to step over them most of the time, but his shoes were soon drenched. His jeans, too, were wet from the grass leaning over the narrow path.

When he reached the point, Joe saw that though the water was well up over the usual fishing spot, someone had thought to rescue the amenities. Several wooden crates had been piled against the base of a tree well above the water-line. Joe set one on its side, put another on end to make a writing surface, and put the lantern on it. The chair crate was too low, he realized when he sat down; his knees were uncomfortably close to his chin. The wood was wet and cold. But he'd spent most of the day wet after all. Maybe that was inevitable if you worked around boats.

He could probably let his aunt and uncle know about his writing, he thought, as he took his legal pad out from under his jacket. They were turning out to be different from his expectations in other ways. Maybe they would accept that as they seemed to accept him. He'd play it by ear. Mean-time, this wasn't so bad after all. It certainly was unique.

He rested the pad against the crate and chewed at the end of his pen for a moment. He still didn't know what he was going to write about his aunt, even exactly what it was about her that made him want to write this sketch. He would just have to start writing and trust himself, as he usually did. He would start by describing her as she had been when he left the boat, overflowing the battered arm-chair, a newspaper hiding her face. Sometimes it worked, sometimes it didn't. He had a feeling, though, that it would work this time.

The darkness seemed to close in around his small light, giving him a sense of solitude, even security. Moths bumped against the glass of the lantern. The sound of the river moved incessantly at the back of his mind. He was getting it. The words were coming almost on their own, in that way they sometimes had, and other thoughts were driven out. Little by little, someone who wasn't quite Myra Essig was coming to life on the page in front of him.

·7·

Amanda was ready to leave, but the number of people outside the house was unnerving. They were clustered around the porch steps by the driveway, chatting with each other, their cameras and sound equipment around them on the grass. James Sterling had gone out to talk to them shortly after they'd arrived, had asked them to move their cars from the drive, and assured them that he would conduct his press conference tomorrow, but they hadn't left. They had moved their cars. It was better than nothing, her father had told her. At least Steve would be able to come up the drive when he picked her up. She had called to warn him about the reporters, and had told him to honk and wait for her in the car.

"Do you want me to go out with you?" her father asked, now. "They would concentrate on me and let you alone."

"That would make it look as if they scare me," Amanda said. "Which they do," she added.

"Just keep moving. If you have to say anything at all, say 'no comment.' And try not to stop. When you stop, they close in around you and it's hard to get moving again."

"Okay."

"And keep in mind that these are just people trying to do their jobs. They aren't out to get you, even if it seems that way."

Amanda squared her shoulders and took a deep breath. "How do I look?"

"Terrific. Athena, ready for battle."

"I thought I was Electra."

"Classical anyway. You're sure you don't want me to go out with you?"

"I'm sure." She opened the door and stepped onto the porch. The effect of her appearance was immediate. People stopped talking, grabbed cameras, picked up their equipment and came closer to the porch steps. It was still light out, but the porch roof and the bushes in front made deep shadows. Lights were switched on. Amanda stood for a moment getting the nerve to start toward them. At least she had a clear stretch of porch for a minute before she reached them. But suddenly a woman with a microphone in her hand came up the steps and onto the porch. As if she had given a signal, the rest followed, and Amanda was surrounded, lights flashing, microphones pushed toward her. Her name was being called by several different voices, and she didn't know where to look. She could see why her father had told her to keep moving. How was she going to go forward with all these people in front of her? What if she took a step and they didn't move? She looked down at her feet, focused on the suede toes of her shoes, and took a step. Then another. People were moving out of the way, some of them stepping backward, others moving sideways. It was like a moving, human tunnel through which she had to walk, trying not to look up. "What do you think about your father's indictment?" "How do you think this will affect the family?" "How are your friends reacting to the news?" The questions were overlapping. It wasn't as hard to ignore them as she'd expected it to be because it was hard to make them out clearly anyway.

To her right she heard a voice repeating her name over

and over. She was almost to the porch steps. Several of the people in front of her were backing down them. She had one brief impulse to give the closest one, that woman who had come onto the porch first, a push. The voice saying her name was getting louder. He seemed just to want to get her to look up. She glanced in the direction of the voice, and a strobe went off directly in her eyes. Dirty trick, she thought, and had to stop. The afterimage of the flash had left her unable to see anything. A huge purple blotch was hanging in front of her and the steps had disappeared. As she waited for the blotch to fade out so she could go on, the same voice asked its question. "How does it feel to know your father could have been responsible for the deaths of your friends? Or your own death? You went to that last basketball game, didn't you?" She looked toward the voice again, wondering what kind of person could ask a question like that. But she still couldn't see well enough to make out faces. This was the kind of question she wanted to be able to answer. If she said "no comment" to this one, or ignored it, wouldn't they think she believed what that creep had said, that her father had knowingly endangered her life? She wished she could come up with a really scathing response, some monumental insult. But she couldn't think of one. The purple was fading. She took the porch steps carefully, looking at her feet again, until she reached the driveway and looked up to see the car and Steve, leaning across from the steering wheel to open the door for her.

She ducked gratefully inside, slamming the door with a force she hoped would crush fingers if anyone was foolish enough to get that close. Steve put the car into reverse, but even as they began to move, the voices followed, questions being called through the open windows. It was like having rocks thrown at her, Amanda thought. She closed her eyes and put her hands over her ears. The car began to move faster and the voices receded.

"So that's what it's like to be a celebrity," Steve said. "They're like those Italian photographers. What are they called?"

"I don't remember." Amanda relaxed and leaned back into her seat. She'd made it. And she hadn't said anything, not even that terrible "no comment."

"Well, you were great, babe." He backed onto River Road, shoved the gearshift forward and took off with a squeal of tires. "What happened when you stopped back there at the edge of the porch? You looked like somebody had smacked you in the face."

"A flash went off in my eyes and I couldn't see for a minute." She didn't feel like repeating the question, or even remembering it.

"You're lucky you didn't fall off the porch."

"I wonder if I could have sued them if I'd broken my leg."

"It's an interesting legal point." He chuckled. "Somehow, I doubt it."

"I'm just glad it's over. I hope they aren't still there when I get back."

"If they are, I'll go into the house with you. I shouldn't have stayed in the car this time."

"Thanks, but there's no sense making you go through that, too. Anyway, Dad says he doesn't think it will go on for too long. He says we just have to batten the hatches and wait it out."

Steve patted her arm. "Politics. Nobody promises you a rose garden. Now you're supposed to forget about all this for a while and remember that you have friends. Lots of them. That's what this party's for."

Amanda looked at Steve, at the familiar profile, the

longish blond hair, the straight nose. This was the person she'd been putting down for playing pinball? This was Steve. He had probably arranged this party, or at least suggested it to Julie, despite the way she'd been avoiding him. He looked back at her. When their eyes met, she felt the warmth in her cheeks. She hadn't been fair. It wasn't his fault her mother was pressuring her. This was the guy who knew almost as much about her as she knew herself. Maybe more.

"What're you thinking about? The reporters?"

"No. As a matter of fact, I was thinking about you."

He grinned and looked back at the road. "It's about time. What were you thinking?"

"Partly that my mother is very anxious to keep us together."

"I always knew there was something I liked about that lady."

"Do your parents say much about me? About us?"

Steve shrugged. "No. But they don't say much to me about anything lately. They're working on some new theory about raising teen-agers. They have a book. I think the main part of the theory is to leave me alone."

"I wish Mom would read that book."

"I could lend it to you. It makes for very quiet dinners. Sometimes I think longingly of the good old days when Dad was trying to mold me into a chip off the old block. At least we talked then—civic responsibility, law school, the joys of public office, all that. I guess I gave him a hard time then, but now that he doesn't do it anymore, I miss it. And poor Mom is always starting to ask something, and then remembering in time to shut up. If it weren't for Jenny, nobody would say anything to anyone from one week to the next. She's refusing to be a teen-ager at all."

Amanda leaned over and kissed Steve on the cheek. "I'm sorry."

"What for?"

"For being such a—I don't know what."

"It's probably just a phase. Maybe you should read that book. I suspect it explains everything. Pavarotti!"

"What?"

"Pavarotti! Those Italian photographers."

"Pavarotti is an opera singer, Stephen," Amanda said.

"Well, it's something like that."

"Pavarotti. I think it *is* something like that. Pa—pa—paparazzi! Isn't that it?"

"Right. Paparazzi. I'm glad we got it—it would have driven me crazy all night. Anyway, I was close."

Amanda laughed. "Pavarotti might not agree with you."

"Here we are, Chez Parnell!" He turned up the winding road between two huge stone gateposts. "Julie warned me that we must not step off the sidewalk. The mud's so bad that three kids and a dog have disappeared in the last week."

The Parnells had lived in their new condominium for nearly six months, but the weather had kept the sod from being put down and the whole project was a sea of mud. Mr. Parnell, who was the developer, was worried, Amanda knew, despite Julie's jokes. The project was built on the bluffs over the river, and there had been several severe mudslides in the last few weeks. Now, with the sun sinking toward the hills downriver, the view from the paved parking lot next to the tall, redwood buildings was breathtaking. The river reflected the sky, blue now for the first time in days, and the orange of the sunlight flashed back toward the hills.

"We seem to be the last ones," Steve said, as he turned off the ignition. The lot was already filled with cars. He kissed Amanda on the nose. "Let's go, babe. Your friends await you."

Julie appeared at the door and waved to them. "Come on in! Everyone's here. We even arranged sunset in your honor!"

Inside, Amanda saw that everyone was indeed there. Between the slate foyer and the glass wall of the living room, overlooking the river, kids were standing, sitting, talking, and eating, and there was a small group gathered around the television screen where an electronic hockey game was in progress. The sliding door that connected the living room with a wide redwood deck was open, and a table was set up outside with pizzas, pop, and half a watermelon filled with fruit. Julie waved toward the deck. "See that elegant watermelon out there? My campers did that. It was all I could think of to have them do today, and then I wouldn't let them eat a bite of it."

Kit came up behind her. "Isn't she rotten? We're going to have to do something for those little cherubs to make up for it."

"Cherubs, ha! Fiends is more like it. You should be with them day after endless rainy day!"

"Has the rain stopped for good do you think?" someone asked. "When will we be able to get the boats out?"

"The sooner the better!" someone answered.

Amanda knew she'd been right to come. There wasn't anything wrong with her, she decided, except that she'd been cooped up for too long.

"Everybody be quiet for a minute," Julie said, and a hush fell over the room so quickly that it had to have been planned. "We all want Amanda to know that no matter what, we're with her, right?"

"Right!" came the answer.

"Thanks," Amanda said. The faces turned toward her

were safe, she thought. Not like the faces behind the lights and microphones.

"So let's forget all about it and have this party!" After the cheer that greeted these words, Julie pulled Amanda out onto the deck and someone turned up the stereo. A couple of people got up to dance.

"Mom and Dad are upstairs," Julie said. "But since there's nobody living next to us yet, they said we didn't have to worry about noise."

"Thanks for this, Julie."

"Listen, what're friends for? I know you'll do the same for me if this whole place slides into the river. Kit was going to have it at her house, but her stepfather has a new rule. No parties and no overnights. Isn't that grim? She considered running away—for about five minutes."

"That's about how long her allowance would last," Steve said as he joined them. "Any beer?"

"Are you kidding? Didn't you hear me say Mom and Dad are upstairs?"

"So where is it?"

"In Mark's car."

"See you later." He turned back at the door. "You coming, Mandy?"

"No thanks. I'll have a Tab."

"Is it safe to dance out here?" one of the guys asked, looking over the edge of the deck, which was built out over the hillside.

"We don't know yet," Julie said. "Tonight will be the test."

"Oh, no it won't. We'll stay inside!"

When Julie went in, Amanda stayed on the deck, watching the sun turn the river to a winding band of orange. There might be a storm at home, she thought, but here the sun was out. After all the rain, the sun was finally out.

91

·8·

When Steve came back, they stayed out on the deck for a while eating pizza, talking about nothing—the weather, movies, music. Eventually, they drifted back into the living room, drawn by the insistent beat of the music. As they started to dance, Amanda had the feeling that it must be like this to be a puppet, to have a will outside yourself moving your arms and legs. The volume of the music, the pulse of it, moved her in spite of herself, washed over and through her. For what seemed a very long time there was nothing in the world, nothing in her mind, except the swirl of color and movement around her and the music itself. It was good to feel her body moving like a smoothly running machine. She gave herself over to it gratefully, Amanda Sterling gone for a while, the machine running without her.

Finally, Steve called a halt and collapsed into a chair. "Time out," he gasped. "I feel like I've just finished four sets of tennis."

Amanda stood by the chair for a moment. She, too, was breathless, her hair stuck to her forehead with perspiration. "Just one more," she begged.

Steve shook his head. "You go ahead. I'm about to die of thirst. When I can move, I'm going outside for a while."

"How about me?" Amanda turned and found Mark, holding his hand out to her. "Kit's someplace with Julie."

And so she was dancing again. But the spell had been broken. She tried to let the music take her, to recapture that sense of freedom, but it wouldn't come. When the music ended, she, too, claimed exhaustion and went to get herself another Tab.

When she came back to the living room, she was just in time to see Steve shake hands with David Lauderbeck, another games fanatic. "Five bucks," David agreed. "Who chooses the game?"

"We could use the Video Olympics cartridge," Steve suggested.

Amanda joined them quickly. "Veto! You'd be at it all night!"

"Don't be a spoilsport," David said. "There are only fifty games on that cartridge."

"Exactly. Veto!" Amanda repeated.

"All right, then, Pong. An oldie but a goodie. Are you going to stay and watch me slaughter this guy?" Steve asked.

Games again, Amanda thought. No matter where they went. "No thanks, I trust you."

"You'd better watch out," David warned. "If he loses, he'll go home broke. Five whole bucks!"

"That's okay," she said. "The drive home isn't expensive."

"Anyway, I never lose!"

As they prepared for their game, Amanda went to sit in a huge leather recliner next to the open sliding doors. Word began to get around that Steve and David were dueling for cash, and the dancing stopped. A crowd gathered around the television screen to watch. She should be there, too,

93

Amanda thought, staring at the droplets of condensation on the can in her hand. Her dislike of the games was becoming as much of an obsession for her as pinball for Steve. But watching them play would hardly change that.

The record ended. Since no one was dancing, no one bothered to put another on. Amanda leaned back, forcing the chair into its reclining position, and closed her eyes, doing her best to shut out the sound of the game, the occasional cheers and shouts of encouragement. She tried to let her mind drift, to let go of conscious thought, as she had been able to do while dancing. Gradually, she became aware of voices behind her. Someone was talking on the deck, just outside the doors. She tried to shut out those sounds as well. But now that she'd become aware of them, it was impossible not to listen.

". . . so why should it surprise anyone?" She recognized the voice. It was Jason King. She had dated Jason for a while before Steve.

"I don't know. But my father was surprised. He really was." Bob McLaughlin. His father was the doctor in charge of the hospital emergency room.

"Why should Sterling be any different?"

Amanda stiffened, nearly knocking over the can she had set on the arm of the chair. Now she was straining backward, determined to hear.

"Because there ought to be somebody who's different, somebody you can trust."

"Hey, we're talking about politics here, not church work. Why do you think people go into politics in the first place?"

"Good question. Why do they?"

"Power, my man. Politics is entirely a power trip. Why else would anybody, anybody who wasn't insane, actually want to be President of the United States, for instance? Except that a word from him could start World War III.

Or set the FBI on somebody he doesn't like. It's the same thing with being mayor, except the stakes are smaller. Anyway, Sterling wants to be governor. I swear to you, it's power."

"Okay. But what does that have to do with whether he's different or not?"

Jason King's voice was impatient. "Because power and money go together, that's why. Power gets money, money gets power."

"In that case, your father ought to be the most powerful man in Grantsport."

Jason laughed. "To hear Mom tell it, he's the devil himself." Jason's family was the oldest banking family in town, and his father had enough money, Amanda knew, to provide Jason with two luxurious homes to choose from when his parents had been divorced. "Anyway, you can't expect a politician to turn down the money that comes with the territory. That's what it's all about, you know, how the whole system works."

Amanda sat up, slamming the chair into its upright position. She didn't want to hear another word. Steve and David were still at their game, hunched over the controls, intent on the screen in front of them. From the hush of their audience, she gathered that the game was a close one. She didn't care. She wanted to get away from here. This safe place had changed. This party wasn't what she'd thought. She went over and stood behind Steve, watching the green blip move back and forth across the screen. She put her hand gently on his head, but he shook it off. "Watch it, you'll break my concentration."

"Sorry."

"Did you decide to come give me moral support?" he asked, without taking his eyes off the screen.

"No. I want to go home."

"Are you kidding?"

"No fair," David said. "There's too much money riding on this game."

"Right," Steve said. "Wait till it's over. Anyway, stick around. I'm just about to get him!"

"I'll be back," Amanda said. Everyone in the living room was intent on the game. She didn't want to go near the deck, didn't want even to see Jason King and Bob Mc-Laughlin. She went into the hall, past the dining room, where Julie and Kit were sitting at the table with a spiral notebook in front of them.

"We need you," Julie called. "We're trying to come up with some new ideas for my campers. I'm wrung dry."

"And I'm rotten at this sort of thing," Kit said.

Amanda pointed to the open door of the bathroom across the hall. "I've got to go to the john."

"Okay. We'll catch you later."

Inside the small pink and gold bathroom, Amanda turned the lock and leaned her forehead against the door. A headache was beginning. A steel band seemed to be tightening around her head. What was this party really about? They were her friends, all right. What she'd seen in their faces when she'd come in hadn't been a lie. But it wasn't what she'd thought, either. These kids were supporting her, not her father. They thought her father was guilty. Now that she'd put the thought into words, its impact was like a blow to her already-aching head.

She ran water into the pink marble sink and held her wrists under the stream, cooling the blood as it pulsed through the veins near the skin. The air was oppressive, as if the house had become a sauna. There were halos around the bathroom lights. It was going to be a really bad headache. She opened the door of the medicine cabinet and found some aspirin. Aspirin probably wouldn't be enough

96

for this one, but she had to do something. She shook two tablets into her hand and filled a glass with the cold water. When the pills had gone down, she finished the water, which seemed, now, almost as warm as the air.

A cheer went up from the living room. The game must be over. They could go. She needed to be with Steve, the only person who could possibly understand. There was no one else she could trust. Not even Kit or Julie. Because she didn't know what any of them thought. And she didn't want to know. If they agreed with Jason, something would be lost; some fundamental part of her life would be changed. How could she relate to people who thought her father was a criminal? There would always be that suspicion underneath. She would wonder what they were thinking when they came to the house.

When she came out of the bathroom, Julie and Kit had joined the others in the living room, where Steve was handing over a five-dollar bill with elaborate ceremony.

"David slays Goliath!" David crowed. "The pinball giant bites the dust!"

"Just come over to my place and see how you do at the real thing," Steve said. "Pong isn't pinball."

"Excuses, excuses."

"I mean it. Let's go to my house right now . . ."

Before David could answer, Amanda put her hand on Steve's arm. "Would you take me home first?" she asked him quietly. "I'm getting a headache."

Steve started to answer, then looked at her more closely. "Okay." He turned back to David. "How about tomorrow? I challenge you to pinball at high noon!"

"You're not leaving already," Julie complained. "You didn't help me with my campers."

"Sorry," Amanda mumbled, but Steve was already guiding her toward the door. She had a feeling he was communicating something to Julie behind her back, but she didn't even care what it was. She just wanted to get out of there.

As they drove down the driveway, Steve turned to look at her. Even in the darkness, she could see the worry on his face. "Are you okay?" he asked. "You look wiped out."

"Just one of my headaches. I think it's going to be a bad one."

"What happened? You seemed okay before."

"I was okay before." She rubbed at her temples. "You're going into politics, right?"

"Right."

"Why?"

"Why?"

"Is it power that appeals to you?"

Stephen frowned and peered ahead, negotiating a curve before he answered. "In a way, I guess. You know, most people don't have much to say about what goes on in the world around them. They have a vote—just that one vote—and that never feels like enough. But if you get yourself into the structure, you have a little control. Yeah, I guess power is most of it. If you don't have the power, you can't do anything about what you believe in."

Amanda nodded. She knew Steve would understand. "Someone has to have the power, after all."

"Right. And if you don't agree with what that person is doing, the best way to fight him is to get the power for yourself."

"So where does money come in?"

Steve began to rub the back of her neck. "How's your head?"

"Okay. That feels good." She sat for a moment, letting his fingers work at the tight knot between her shoulders. "But what about money?"

98

"You mean what's the connection between power and money?"

"Yes."

"Listen. This party was supposed to get your mind off what happened today. What is this, a philosophical crisis?"

"I guess it is." She told him about the conversation she'd overheard, but not about her reaction. She didn't have to explain that to Steve.

"Jason's pretty much right, I suppose. You can't do much of anything without money. Not just politicians, either. Lobby groups have to have plenty of money, too. It's all a kind of buying-and-selling game, if you want to look at it that way."

"Anyone who does look at it that way would automatically assume that Dad's guilty, wouldn't they? They'd have trouble understanding that for some people the power is more important than money."

Steve shrugged. "Money *is* important, though. To your father as much as to anybody. You don't get power without it. The governorship doesn't come cheap, any more than the presidency does."

Amanda shook her head. "No. What I mean is that they don't understand that even if money's important, for some people honesty is more important."

Stephen didn't answer. He went on rubbing the back of her neck, but there seemed to be a difference suddenly, as if he had somehow moved away from her. The car's headlights glinted off puddles along the side of the road. As the silence between them stretched on, Amanda felt the band around her head tighten another notch. "Stephen?" Still he didn't respond. "You agree with them, don't you? You think Dad took that bribe?"

Steve stopped the car at a red light and took his hand away to shift gears. "I don't know how to answer that,

99

Mandy. A grand jury has to have pretty much evidence to bring an indictment against the mayor." The light changed, and he pulled away with a jerk. "I admire your father very much, babe. I don't want to jump to any conclusions."

Amanda swallowed hard. It felt as if the aspirins were lodged in her windpipe. "How can you even think he might do such a thing? Would you think your father had done it if the indictment had been against him?"

"I wouldn't want to think so. But how could I be sure? They are human, Mandy."

"Stop!" Amanda took hold of the door handle beside her. "Stop the car."

Steve didn't even slow down. "Take it easy, babe. I just . . ."

"I said, stop the car. If you don't, I'm going to jump out while it's moving, I swear I will."

Steve put on the brakes and pulled over to the curb. They were on River Road, but still nearly a quarter of a mile from her house. "Now listen to me . . ."

She opened the door and stepped out. "See you," she said.

"Amanda!" he called, leaning across the seat. "Get back in here."

She slammed the door and began walking along the shoulder of the road. Steve pulled up next to her. "Get back in here! I didn't mean . . ."

"I know exactly what you meant." She kept walking, stepping into a puddle she hadn't seen.

"I'll get out and drag you back into the car," Steve warned.

"And I'll get right back out again. What'll you do, tie me up?"

"Come on, Mandy. Don't do this." He kept the car moving just enough to stay abreast of her.

"Go home, Stephen."

"Amanda!"

She didn't answer. She just kept walking, concentrating on putting one foot in front of the other, each step jolting through her head. Finally, Steve tapped his horn lightly. "Okay, you win. But I'll be over to see you in the morning." She didn't look toward him. "Be careful!"

The car swept past her and she watched until it was out of sight around the curve. No sooner had the taillights disappeared than she felt like an idiot. What was the point? Now she was walking along a dark road full of puddles, her head pounding, her shoes wet, having proved nothing except how stubborn she could be. She hadn't realized how dark it was along here at night. She was always in a car, and there were always the headlights. As she came to the curve, she could see a streetlight far ahead. But here the long sloping lawns on her right were dotted with big old trees, the leaves a thick canopy of even deeper darkness. Lights from the Victorian houses on the slopes above her made the darkness here, along the road, even worse. And across the road, on the river side, a tangle of bushes and weeds came all the way to the shoulder. Plenty of places for someone to hide, she thought, and then almost laughed. What was she afraid of? Murderers? Muggers? Rapists? Yes, she admitted, all of those. She began to walk more quickly, ignoring the puddles, heading for that comforting pool of light around the base of the streetlight ahead. Finally, she was there. She wished she could just stay there, in the light, and someone she knew would come along. But then she imagined someone hiding in the darkness, watching her. It was a crazy thought, but she couldn't shake it. She didn't want to stay in the light after all, so visible. So vulnerable.

She kept on walking, getting more and more angry with

herself, but at the same time, more and more aware of shadows and sounds. Just one more streetlight. It wasn't much farther now. Just one more easy bend. She stopped. Parked at the base of the hill in front of her house was a Volkswagen beetle. What was it doing there? Surely, the reporters weren't still waiting outside the house. Why would anyone still be there at this hour? She couldn't see whether anyone was in the car or not, but she stepped off the road. If there were someone in the car, she didn't want to be seen. She couldn't stand going through the lights and cameras again. Not after the party. And worse, she didn't want anyone to know she was coming home on foot. Then it wouldn't just be reporters' questions, but her parents' questions she'd have to cope with. She could imagine telling her mother that she'd forced Steve to let her walk home.

She could go up the hill from where she was, and cut across the yards and go in the back door. But there would still be questions from her parents. Why hadn't Steve driven up the drive? Why hadn't he come in with her? Despite her headache, despite her wet feet, she was not going to be able to go home. Not yet. But what would she do instead?

There was the Peg. If it had been a good idea this afternoon, it was even better now. The boat would be cozy and private, infinitely less frightening than being out here alone on the road. But if she went to the Peg, she'd have to put on the lights, and then the Essigs would come to investigate. Or worse, they might send their nephew. She'd almost rather take her chances with whoever was in the VW than face Joe Schmidt again, mocking her, wanting to know what she was doing at the boat at this hour.

Wherever she went, she'd have to stay long enough to give the person in the beetle time to give up and leave, and her parents time to go to bed. They didn't always wait up for her when she was with Steve. There was a place by the river she used to go when she was too young to drive the boat, even before she was allowed to paddle around the marina in the dingy. A huge old tree had fallen over, its trunk split by lightning, the inside empty and blackened by fire. It was big, dry inside, almost like a cave. She'd gone there whenever she wanted to be alone, and sometimes spent a whole afternoon inside that tree. It was probably underwater now, with the river so high. But the thought of that old refuge, of being close to the river, made her feel better. There was an access road that led down to the river between her house and the marina. The fallen tree wasn't far from that road.

Amanda peered ahead, trying to see if anyone was in the Volkswagen. It was too dark to tell. If she couldn't see into the car, though, anyone in the car wouldn't be able to see her. She ran across the road and into the weeds, trying not to think about hiding rapists. Actually, on this side of the road she was somehow less frightened of the dark. This side of the road belonged to the river, not to people. However foolish it was, this side felt safer. It was her river, after all.

When she came even with the Volkswagen, moving slowly, well back into the bushes, she saw that there was someone inside, but he was facing toward the house, the back of his head against the window. Must be the world's most boring job, she thought. And ugly, like spying.

She went on, pushing her way through the bushes, brambles catching at her jeans. Amazingly enough, her headache was letting up a little. Maybe the aspirins were working after all. At last she reached the access road, scarcely more than two narrow ruts, nearly obscured by the tall grass. If she hadn't known it was there, she'd never have found it. She paused for a moment before starting down it toward the river. Where would she go if her fallen tree really was underwater? There was the point where Ryan Creek met the river. Fishermen kept something there to sit on. She could always go there.

Overhead, the stars were out, clear, bright pinpoints in the blackness. There was no moon. Ducking under a rangy sumac that leaned across the road, she walked directly into a wet spider web. From then on, she kept one hand in front of her face. She reached the line of tall trees and went in among them. Suddenly, the road ended in the water. Ahead, the willow scrub continued, the dark shapes seeming to get shorter until they disappeared, yards out where the beach would normally be. Her fallen tree was clearly under water. It had been only a short way from the beach. It would have to be the point, then. She started to her right, slipping in the mud occasionally, tripping over a fallen branch, or stepping into a hole from time to time, but the footing wasn't as bad as it could be. She hoped someone had thought to be sure whatever they kept at the point to sit on had been moved up away from the water. She wanted to be able to sit down when she got there, to sit and be alone with the river.

By the time she saw the light, it was too late to turn back or to keep from being seen. She'd been making a terrible racket and already the dark figure between her and the light was standing, peering in her direction. "Who's there?" a voice called out. Now the figure was moving toward her. She checked the impulse to run. After all, whoever this was had a light. If it were a rapist or murderer, he'd hardly advertise himself that way.

"Who's there?" the voice came again, and she recognized it. It was him—Joe Schmidt. Amanda felt like kicking herself. First, she'd jumped out of Steve's car like a lunatic, and now she was here, practically at the end of the world, practically in the middle of the night, alone again with Joe Schmidt.

"It's me," she said. "Amanda Sterling. I didn't expect to find anyone down here."

·9·

"I hadn't exactly expected to have a party here myself," Joe answered, cursing whatever quirk of fate had brought Amanda Sterling, of all people, to this godforsaken bit of mud just at this moment. He stood where he was, acutely aware of the legal pad on the crate behind him. What could he say about why he was here? And what was she doing here? Maybe, he thought hopefully, she'll just go away.

Amanda couldn't decide whether to go ahead, onto the point of land where Joe was standing, or to turn around and take her chances with the reporter and her parents. So she didn't move. Maybe this whole evening was a nightmare, she thought, and she would wake up and find herself in bed. Maybe this whole day was a nightmare. The fishy, dead smell of the river in flood washed over her. That was real, all right.

"We've got to stop meeting like this," Joe said.

"Very funny." Still neither of them moved. Was he down here with a girl? Maybe he was a drug addict, here to shoot heroin or something.

"Well, you might as well come out of the trees, unless you're going to go back the way you came."

Amanda stayed where she was. "What are you doing down here?" she asked.

106

Joe sighed. Obviously, she was not going to magically disappear. "Practicing my secret vice."

"Oh, God," Amanda muttered and stepped backward.

"You don't have to run," Joe said. "I'm not a grave robber or anything."

"What are you, then? You can't be working on an engine down here."

"You certainly take a narrow view of people."

"That's not an answer. What are you doing here?" He answered but she couldn't make out what he'd said. His voice had dropped almost to nothing. "What?"

"I said writing. Writing! You know, with pencil and paper?"

If he had told her he was burying a dismembered body, Amanda could not have been more surprised. "Writing?" She emerged from the trees and came into the light from his lantern. Her white jeans were wet and muddy, her hair tangled, her arms marked with the long red streaks of bramble scratches. "Writing what?"

"Until I was so rudely interrupted, I was working on a character sketch."

Amanda realized that her mouth was open and closed it. "Creative writing, you mean?"

"Sometimes it's more creative than others." Joe was beginning to feel that old hostility again. Would she be standing there in shock if she'd found one of her friends writing? "I *can* put words on paper. Sometimes I even spell them properly."

"You don't have to be so touchy. Nobody accused you of being illiterate. But you have to admit that writing character sketches in the dark by the river is just a little unusual."

"No more than taking walks in the dark, through the mud and the brambles."

"We weren't talking about me." Amanda looked toward the crates he'd been using. "Are we going to stand here trading insults or what? I'd rather sit down, if you don't mind."

Joe didn't move for a moment. This was hardly the response he'd expected. But as long as he was here with Amanda Sterling, poison or not, he might as well make the best of it. "Excuse me. I warned you that our side of the family lacks manners." He removed the lantern from the upright crate and gestured to the other. "I hope you'll find my desk chair comfortable."

Amanda sat gingerly on the damp wood. "Very nice. The upholstery is lovely."

"Thank you." He picked up the legal pad and sat down on the other crate. "The office came already furnished. I'm particularly fond of the dead fish."

Amanda laughed. What in the world was she doing here, laughing with Joe Schmidt? And how was Joe Schmidt making her laugh? How had he managed to change so completely from that hostile, mocking person she'd met this morning. "What kinds of things do you write?"

"Whatever comes. Poems sometimes. Usually short stories." When he looked at her, she recognized his eyes. They were the eyes from her dream. "Are you impressed?" he asked.

"What? Impressed?" She was thrown for a moment by those eyes. Why had Joe Schmidt's eyes been a part of her dream? "Do you write to impress people?"

Joe thought about his father. "Hardly."

They sat there, then, without speaking, not looking at each other. They were suddenly acutely aware of the place, the river, the damp crates. "What are *you* doing down here?" Joe asked.

"Taking a walk."

"Alone? Without a light? In the mud?"

Amanda stared at the river. He wouldn't understand. If Steve hadn't, how could anyone else. She rubbed at one of the scratches on her arm. She hadn't even noticed getting it.

"I'm sorry," Joe said.

"For what?"

"For asking, I suppose. It's none of my business. But I'm sorry for this morning, too." He could hardly believe he had seen her for the first time that morning. Amanda Sterling seemed by now to have been a part of his consciousness for a very long time. "I hadn't heard about the indictment yet."

Amanda continued to stare across the wide expanse of water. "I hadn't either." She didn't want to talk about this.

"My uncle really had told me the story, but he said it wasn't anything. I wouldn't have mentioned it if I'd known how serious it was."

Amanda met his eyes and remembered the menace from her dream. "Why did you? Why did you let me think your uncle had been talking about my father that way?"

Now Joe looked away. How could he answer that question in a way she would understand. A moth was bumping into the lantern glass again. It was a handy symbol, like himself, always on the other side of an invisible wall from something he wanted, always crashing into it. "Do you really want to know?"

"I asked."

"All right. But I don't know if I can really explain. I wanted to upset you. Get you off-balance."

"Why did you want to do that?" Not that it had been hard, she thought. She'd been off-balance from the moment he'd spoken to her.

Joe ran a hand through his hair and watched the moth, crashing, fluttering, crashing again. "It was mainly because you're rich."

"Me? Rich?" Amanda laughed. "Rich?"

"According to my definition. Nobody but a rich kid drives a car like yours or has a cabin cruiser or wears those alligator shirts."

Amanda glanced down at the symbol on her shirt. "Everybody wears those." Joe just looked at her. "Even if I were rich, which I'm not, what does that explain?"

So Joe tried to tell her what it was like to be dismissed, to be typed by appearance, then ignored, looked through, patronized. And about his determination, when someone did that to him, to insist on being seen.

"Did I do that to you?" she asked, trying to remember. All she knew clearly was that she'd been frightened. Which is what he'd wanted.

Joe nodded. "You saw a boat mechanic, and that was that."

Amanda looked at his clothes, at his battered shoes, his too-long hair. "But that's exactly what you wanted me to see. You're costumed for the part."

Joe looked down at his shoes, at the holes, his bare feet showing through. "I *am* a mechanic. I don't dress up for work."

"That doesn't explain your hair," she pointed out.

"My hair?"

"None of the guys you call rich wear their hair that long. They haven't for ages. Think about who wears their hair that way now."

Was she right? Joe wondered. He didn't want to be typed that way, but maybe he did some things that invited the treatment he hated so. "Okay, so I make an effort to fit into my class."

110

"Has it ever occurred to you that you're a snob?"

"*I'm* a snob?"

Amanda nodded. "You think in terms of money. And class. For yourself and for everybody else. You don't like being typed, but that's exactly what you did to me. You saw my car and the boat and deliberately set out to scare me."

"No I didn't. Not at first, anyway. The truth is . . ." He paused. He was certainly not going to tell her why he'd followed her in the first place. "Never mind. I can only say that I didn't intend to do what I did until I saw the way you looked at me."

"Then I apologize too. Does that make us even?"

"Even. Not equal."

"That is some major hang-up you have."

"It's well earned."

A silence fell between them again. Amanda wondered if the reporter had left yet, and if her parents had gone to bed. The night was warm enough, but her feet were getting cold. They were probably wrinkled by now, as if she'd been soaking in the bathtub. But she was sure it was still too early to go home. Now she'd have to explain her appearance, too.

Joe watched Amanda shift on the crate, rub at her arms again. What was she doing down here? Whatever had sent her stumbling through the mud must have been rough. And it probably had to do with her father. He had denied his aunt's description of Amanda as pretty earlier, but he could see what she'd meant. It wasn't entirely how she looked, but who she was. There was a toughness to her that was even more appealing than her freckles. She looked up at him now, and he looked away, embarrassed to be caught staring again, this time for a very different reason.

"Why did you say writing was your secret vice?"

Joe dropped the legal pad onto his lap. Amanda Sterling wouldn't think writing a waste of time, of course. In her world wanting to be a writer would be admirable, probably. What could she understand of a father like his, or a world like his? If he was a snob, as she'd said, who was it he didn't accept, her kinds of people or his own? "It's a long story," he said at last.

"I'm not on a tight schedule," she said.

Joe rested his elbows on his knees and looked at the water's edge. A plastic milk jug bumped against the mud, surrounded by greenish brown foam and a litter of twigs. He would tell her the story, he decided, as if he were writing it; he would make her see his world, his family, himself. He cleared his throat, and began with his family.

As he talked, he realized little by little that he was telling the story of Joe Schmidt not so that Amanda Sterling would understand, but so that he would. Hearing his words spoken aloud like that, he began to see more clearly how he felt, why he felt the way he did. Amanda was sitting very still, leaning forward as if she actually cared about what he was saying. The sound of the river blended with his voice, and he talked on and on, painting a picture of his isolation, almost as if he were talking about someone else.

When he came to the morning his father had refused to sign the form, though, he felt the fury rising in him, and stopped. If he went on, he was afraid he would choke on that fury. In the silence, he heard the soft thumping again. Two moths were now circling the lantern and diving vainly at its cold, bluish light. Suddenly it wasn't fury. Suddenly, underneath his anger was pain. It washed over him in a flood, and he could only sit there, swallowing and staring at his footprint in the mud in front of him. Had there been a time, ever in his life, when he'd known for sure that his father was proud of him? Had anything he'd done, any of the honors and awards he'd won, ever meant anything to his father?

Amanda looked at the person who only that morning had seemed so threatening. His fists were clenched, his knuckles white, almost raw looking in the lantern light. She *was* rich, she realized, according to his standards. And he was alien. There was nothing about the family he had described that she could relate to. What would it be like, she wondered, to have a baby and go to work instead of going back to school for her junior year? She couldn't even imagine it.

But in other ways, Joe Schmidt was not so very different. Right now, she knew, he was hurting. Just as Doug and Steve could tell about her headaches, she could see the pain in every line of his body. She wanted to say something, to offer some kind of comfort, but she couldn't. She was too far from understanding what was causing such pain. So she waited.

Finally, Joe spoke again, and the rest of the story fell into place. "So I'm effectively an orphan," he concluded. "Stuck between two worlds."

"And hating them both."

Joe looked up. "What?"

"I said, hating them both. Don't you?" He didn't answer. "You don't seem to like anybody very much."

Joe stood up and went to the water's edge, kicking at the empty milk carton. It floated out, then back against the line of dirty foam. She hadn't understood. Why should it surprise him? How could a pampered princess, a mayor's daughter, the apple of her father's eye, no doubt, ever understand?

Amanda watched him, wishing she hadn't said what she'd said. Obviously, it had been the wrong thing. It certainly hadn't offered any comfort. But it was what she'd felt as she'd listened to his story. He seemed to be full of resentment, even bitterness. He wasn't really very likable. Why did she find herself liking him? Obviously, he didn't return the feeling. She stood up. "Well, I guess I'll see you around the marina."

"Are you going?"

"My schedule has suddenly become tight."

He turned back to her. When their eyes met, she had the sensation of the dream again. "I want you to know," he said, "that I've never told anyone what I just told you. In case you think I'm in the habit of complaining about my hard life."

"I didn't think that."

"I'll consider what you said. Just so you know I heard you." He smiled.

Even at the edge of the lantern's pale light, Amanda could see that the smile had changed his whole face. That's why I like him, she thought, because he's more than one person. And not like anyone I know.

"Would you like me to walk you home?" he asked.

Amanda looked at her watch. It wasn't as late as she'd hoped. "Actually, my schedule has loosened up again." She looked up at the stars. "There's the Big Dipper."

"And the summer triangle. Deneb, Vega, Altair."

"Not you too!" she said, trying to see what he was looking at. "The dipper is the only thing I can ever find, except the Pleiades. Doug—my brother—despairs of me. He knows them all, of course."

"I only know a few," Joe admitted. "There's Cassiopeia and there's Andromeda. My sign would be somewhere over there." He pointed across the river. "Sort of behind the Kentucky hills."

"What is your sign?"

114

"Sagittarius. What's yours? Why are you laughing?"

"It figures, that's all. I'm a Scorpio. Sagittarius and Scorpio are deadly enemies."

They both laughed, looked at each other, and laughed again. Suddenly their being together on this stretch of mud, their feet wet, the flood current rushing by, struck them both as hilarious. Amanda sank back down onto the crate, wiping her eyes. "Maybe we're both crazy."

Joe nodded. "You know why I'm crazy enough to be out here. Are you willing to tell me now why you are?"

"All right," she said. "But there isn't much to say. It isn't really important."

"Do unimportant things often drive you down to the river in the middle of the night?"

"I used to come down when I was little, to a big hollow tree. It was kind of a safe place. It's under water now."

"You knew it would be, didn't you?"

Amanda shrugged. "I guess so. I don't want to talk about it."

"Hardly the same as saying it isn't important." Joe had an impulse to put his hand on her shoulder, but he didn't. "Why did you want a safe place?"

Amanda shrugged. Would Joe think what the others thought? Did it matter?

"Is it about your father?" he asked.

She nodded. "I was at a party. I ran away, and then didn't want to go home because there was a reporter there. I didn't want to go past reporters again." Joe was standing too close, Amanda thought. If she was going to be able to tell him anything, she couldn't have him so close that she was aware of him every minute. "Wouldn't you like to sit down again?"

"Okay."

She made her voice as light as she could. "They think my father's guilty. My friends do. But he isn't, so it doesn't really have to concern me."

"You ran away over something that doesn't concern you?"

Amanda wondered if he was mocking her again. It was hard to tell with him. "I just can't stand people judging him when they don't know him." She shook her head slowly. "It's like what you were talking about, the way people judge other people by appearances. Except it's much worse in politics."

"Politicians know that before they ever get into that life, don't they?" Joe had never understood why a man would want a life of having to go back to the people over and over to win enough votes to keep his job.

"Dad knew it, but he's never liked it much. What makes me so mad is that the very same people who called him a good mayor six months ago are saying he's bad now. He hasn't changed. And they don't know any more about him, either. They've just switched labels."

"Maybe the real trouble is that 'good' and 'bad' aren't real, applied to a person. Nobody's just one or the other."

Amanda stood up. "My father is. He's good. It's as simple as that."

Nothing is as simple as that, Joe thought. But he didn't say it. Clearly, Amanda would not want to hear any more doubts. "Are you ready to go home?" Amanda nodded. "Then, Miss Sterling, may I have the honor of walking with you? If the reporter's still there, we'll either face him together or give him the slip."

Amanda hoped her parents had either gone to bed or somehow wouldn't notice how she looked. "Okay. My feet are cold."

"Mine too." Joe carried the lantern between them, and they went back the way Amanda had come. It was an easier walk with a light, Amanda thought. She wondered what Joe had thought when she'd come stumbling through the darkness at him. He'd probably been as scared as she was. Now that the rain had stopped, the lightning bugs had come out, blinking high in the trees. Amanda wondered if Joe had caught lightning bugs in a mayonnaise jar when he was little, if he'd made a night-light for his room. She didn't even know if he'd had a room of his own to make a night-light for. Had he ever come out so late that the lightning bugs were all as high as they were now, out of reach? It had happened to her sometimes, and she'd cried. Had Joe cried about lightning bugs? As she listened to the frogs, and to the squelch of their shoes in the mud, she realized that she had never known a person whose life had been so different from her own.

Amanda wasn't anything he'd expected her to be, Joe thought as he walked, intensely aware of her nearness. Once, as she reached up to move a branch out of the way, her hand brushed his, and the touch left an afterimage like a burn. He wondered if she really didn't know she was rich. Could a person live with the kinds of advantages she had and not even notice? When she was ready to go to college, it would be no more to her family than buying her another alligator shirt, or at least no more than another car. And here he was, facing two and a half years of working just to get to the starting point. Even then, he'd probably have to borrow to finish graduate school, and would have to start out with that debt hanging over him. He ought to resent her and everything she stood for. Instead, he kept remembering the look on her face, so pale in the lantern light, when she'd tried to pretend that what her friends thought about her father didn't bother her.

They reached River Road and Amanda pointed to the right. "It's that way. Not very far."

"Can you tell if anyone's there?"

"The VW is."

Joe switched off the lantern. In the sudden darkness, he thought again that he had underestimated Amanda. She had come this way by herself, down this road in the dark. Hardly what one would expect of a pampered princess. She was probably right about him. He, too, judged by appearances. "I'll leave the lantern here and get it on my way back. Should we cross here?"

"Yes. And cut up through the yards."

Joe took her hand and they ran across River Road and up onto the lawn three houses down from the Sterlings'. "You'll have to lead from here," he said. "This is definitely not my territory."

She went ahead, pulling him after her. When they reached the hedge around her backyard, she giggled. "What?" Joe whispered.

"Promise you won't be offended."

"I never make a promise I'm not sure I can keep."

"I was just thinking about what my mother would say if she saw me out here sneaking around in the bushes with you."

Joe laughed. "I don't think my mother would much like the idea, either."

Joe was so close to her, Amanda could feel his breath on her cheek. She stepped back, pulled her hand from his and went through the hedge. He followed, whistling softly when he saw the house. Lights were on all over the first floor. "And you say you aren't rich?"

"I said you were a snob," she said. "The floors warp in the summer and the fuses blow all the time."

"Isn't it just awful!"

"You can be a real pain, you know?"

They stood for a moment, looking at each other. "You're wet," he said. "How are you going to explain that? And all those scratches?"

"I don't know," Amanda admitted. "Maybe we had a scavenger hunt at the party? In the mud?"

"Not bad. I'd offer to go inside with you, but I suspect that wouldn't help."

Amanda giggled again. "No. That wouldn't help."

"Will you be okay?"

"Sure. And thanks. I didn't want to come back by myself."

"You're welcome." Joe found himself wanting to thank her, too. Instead, before he had a chance to think what he was doing, he took her by the shoulders, pulled her toward him and kissed her. Then he backed away. "I'll see you at the marina."

Amanda nodded. She seemed to be having trouble breathing. She turned away and ran up the steps to the back door. When she looked back, he had disappeared through the hedge again. She stood at the door for a moment, getting her breath, trying to prepare herself for her mother's questions. A *scavenger hunt outside the condominiums. Stephen had let her out of the car and she'd come around through the yards to avoid the guy in the Volkswagen.* It would have to do.

When she opened the door, she heard her parents' voices, loud, grating, unpleasant. She hadn't heard them yelling at each other more than a few times in her life. Almost immediately they stopped. How had they heard her over the noise they were making? The silence seemed almost tangible, worse than the yelling had been. "Is that you, Amanda?" her mother's voice was tight, falsely bright.

"Yes. Just me." Her voice sounded exactly like her

mother's. "I've got a headache," she said, and for once it was a lie. "I'll just go on up to bed."

"Good night," her father called. He didn't seem to be coming into the kitchen.

"Good night," she said, and slipped up the back stairs, grateful that she wouldn't have to pass them and explain anything. In her room, she sank onto her bed and untied her shoes. As she took them off, she realized that even stranger than the yelling was the fact that neither of them, not even her mother, had asked a single question.

·10·

That night was only the beginning of the strangeness at home. In the next few days, while June began to seem more like June, sunny and hot and muggy, the Sterlings seemed to continue to live under clouds. Even when the river quit rising, a few days after the rain stopped, and the water level at last began to fall, Amanda had the sense that in her family the water was still rising, and flood was still a danger.

James Sterling had held his promised news conference the next day, but had failed to satisfy the press. He had merely promised that a trial would prove his innocence and had refused to answer the charges. The headlines, "Sterling's Name Tarnished," and "Sterling Character Questioned," were replaced with "Mayor Refuses Comment." Despite her father's advice, Amanda found it hard to ignore the papers and impossible to stay away from both television and radio.

Since the yelling, something was different about the way her parents behaved. They didn't go on yelling, but they didn't speak to each other as much as usual either. And there seemed to be unspoken arguments going on between them. She would catch one of them looking at the other, and she would look away herself, unable to interpret the meanings. When her mother fixed dinner, or put the food on the table, she seemed to be practically throwing the dishes around, putting them down so hard sometimes that it seemed a bowl or a glass might break. She would ask Amanda to set the table, or Doug to fix a salad, as usual, but then she didn't talk to them, even though they were working there in the kitchen with her.

Steve had called the day after the party, but Amanda had told Doug to say she had a headache and couldn't talk. Ever since, she had stayed in the house, reading, listening to records, waiting for the river to go down so she could get out on the Peg. When one of the kids called, she made an excuse. Once, when Steve came to the house, she had locked herself in her room and even refused to speak to him through the door. And through it all, her mother asked no questions, made no suggestions, didn't even seem to notice.

Amanda didn't see Joe either, though she often thought of going down to the marina just to see if he was there, to see what he was doing. In fact, she found herself thinking about him almost continually, and was grateful that her mother had quit paying attention to her. She couldn't explain even to herself how she felt about Joe Schmidt, or what had happened that night, or why. She had hoped, for a while, that he would call her, and then decided that he probably wasn't even thinking about her. They were impossibly different. He would probably prefer to stay well away from her and everything she symbolized. Probably that kiss had been no more significant than a handshake. It hadn't been particularly romantic, after all.

Doug seemed the least affected either by the publicity or by the change in the Sterlings' behavior. While he was quieter than usual, less ready with a wisecrack, less determined to share his enthusiasm about his projects, he went right on with those projects. If he wasn't in his room with his books, he was out somewhere working on a method for predicting changes in the river level.

Four days after the press conference, Amanda woke early and found her parents arguing again. She had slipped into shorts and a halter and had started down the back stairs to the kitchen, when she became aware of their voices and stopped. "It's the second time this week," her mother was saying. "You are going to have to do something—make some kind of statement. This silence has convinced everyone you're guilty! More and more people are demanding that you resign!"

"You don't know that, Peg. Believe me, I have a better handle on what's happening downtown than you do. These women's groups have absolutely no way of knowing what's going on."

"Then why have they canceled those meetings where I was to speak? They haven't the guts to tell me they don't want to hear me, so they've canceled entirely. But I know what it means."

"You know what it means in terms of those women. There isn't any connection between them and the reality of my position at this moment. They're reading the crap in the papers and listening to the evening news. How else would you expect them to react?"

Peg Sterling's voice broke as she began to speak. There was a pause, and then she began again. "So why don't you fight that? Did you read Edelson's piece last night? That quotation from Robert Browning—'Just for a handful of silver he left us. Just for a riband to wear on his coat.' He doesn't question your guilt for a minute. He doesn't seem to need proof. When people read that kind of thing, they believe it, Jim! And the longer you keep quiet, the more sure they are you've got something to hide."

So that was the problem, Amanda thought. Her mother

123

wanted him to deny the charges and he wouldn't. She was amazed to discover that for once she agreed with her mother.

"Peg, there is no point in going on with this argument. I understand that right now this thing is messing up your life. What can I say? It isn't exactly roses for me either. But I *am* right. No defense I use will be enough to get them off my back. Silence at least lets it fade out on its own. It will be months before the case gets into a courtroom, and then we'll be able to handle it. In the meantime, I'm not going to resign. An indictment is not a conviction, and we're reminding people of that all the time. When people realize the city is still running, the furor will die down. Dyer just got a new contract—since this whole thing broke. There are people out there who can keep some perspective."

"Dyer gets contracts, I get canceled." There was a crash, as Peg Sterling apparently threw something down and left the kitchen. Amanda slipped back into her room and waited until she heard her parents' bedroom door slam. By the time she got down to the kitchen, her father had gone.

On the stove was a pan of scrambled eggs. The cup at her father's place was half-full of coffee. Amanda sat down and sipped at her father's coffee, trying to sort out what she had just heard. While she agreed with her mother that his silence implied guilt, she could see her father's point, too. What was the most unsettling in everything he had said, was that Dyer could go on constructing buildings when no one knew yet whether he had purposely allowed the gym to be built unsafely. Who would contract with Dyer now? And why?

Doug appeared in the archway, still in his pajamas. He looked his age, for a change. His hair was tousled and damp around his face, his pajamas were rumpled, his bare feet looked very small. She had an impulse to hug him, but he was too far away. "Poor Mom," he said. "This is harder on her than anybody."

"Why do you think that? It's only a couple of canceled speeches, for heaven's sake," Amanda said, thinking that her father's whole career was on the line.

Doug shook his head. "It must be some sort of natural law that teen-age girls and their mothers can't understand each other. Sometimes I think you two inhabit different planets."

"All right, what do you understand that I don't?"

"Didn't you see her yesterday? She spent the entire day in slacks and a T-shirt. She never put on her makeup, or even combed her hair. Mandy, didn't you notice?"

Amanda shrugged. "I spent the day in my room with a Gothic novel."

Doug dished the scrambled eggs onto a plate and sat down. "Besides that, we haven't had a homemade cookie, brownie, or pie since the day the indictment was announced. Baking is Mom's safety valve. If she isn't using the safety valve, there is going to be some big bang."

Was he right? Amanda wondered. Was all that homebody stuff a safety valve? "What do you know?"

"Not much." Doug spoke around a mouthful of eggs. "Not anything, really. But I've been watching, and Dad hasn't changed all that much. Mom has. And you, of course. But you've been changing for ages. I assume that is some nasty part of being sixteen I have to look forward to."

"All right, maybe Mom's having a hard time. Maybe we all are. But what are we supposed to do about it?"

"Nothing, I guess. How could we do anything? Mom and Dad have to work it out between themselves." He swallowed the last of his eggs. Amanda got up and poured a glass of orange juice for each of them. "You know," Doug said, taking the glass she offered him, "what's going on with us is a little like what has happened to life forms all over the world, right from the beginning."

Amanda groaned. Doug could work fossils into any subject on earth.

As usual, he ignored her reaction. "Most forms of life haven't been able to think or to control their lives in any way. They just eat and rest and reproduce—if they're lucky. Then along comes some great change. Like an ice age. Or some new form of life that happens to want to eat them. It could be anything. Something outside them, sometimes not even related to them at all, changes. Then they either have to adapt to that change, sometimes pretty fast, or they die out. I've been thinking that the same thing is happening to us. Six months ago, we were just us, living the same kind of life we've always lived. We're some of the lucky ones, you know. And then something outside changed—the roof fell down—and we're scrambling to adapt."

"How does it look for us?" she asked. "Are we on the way out?"

Doug sat looking at his empty plate for a moment. When he looked up, his eyes were old again in his little boy's face. "I don't know, Mandy. It could be."

The rest of the morning Amanda spent in her room again, finishing the novel she'd begun the day before. Doug fixed himself some sandwiches and went off, carrying his canvas bag. Around noon, Amanda went to the closed door of her mother's room and considered knocking, asking if she wanted to have some lunch. But her mother was talking on the phone, so she fixed herself an omelet and ate alone, instead. It was probably just as well. Even if Doug was right, Amanda wasn't likely to be able to offer

126

any help. They would probably have ended their lunch with another fight. Neither of them needed that.

Putting her dishes in the sink, Amanda decided to go to the library. Until the river went all the way down to normal, she would just stay inside and read. On the way to the library, she remembered the quotation her mother had mentioned—from a poem by Robert Browning. While she was there, she could look up the poem and see what the point of it was. "A handful of silver," repeated itself over and over in her mind. Whatever the poem was about, she already hated that phrase. First, using it had been another cheap trick with their name, but worse than that, it radiated betrayal, like Judas's thirty pieces of silver.

In the library, she passed the new-book table without a glance and went straight to the English poetry and drama shelves. As she scanned the contents of a volume of Browning's work, she realized that she didn't know the title of the poem she was looking for. Hoping the quotation was from the beginning, she looked in the index of first lines and found it. She took the book to a table where an old man was hunched over a newspaper, and sat down with it.

The poem, "The Lost Leader," was terrible, she decided. Overdramatic. A footnote explained that it had probably been written about Wordsworth, who had been a liberal and had become a conservative. She almost laughed out loud. Did people ever get that excited about a political philosophy? "Blot out his name, then, record one lost soul more," it said. Lost soul? "One wrong more to man," he called Wordsworth's conversion, "One more insult to God!" With an exclamation point, yet. Obviously, the columnist had chosen the first two lines for the apparent connection to her father. But the rest of the poem was worthless. She closed the book with a bang, and the old man across the table from her snapped his paper testily and frowned at her before putting it in front of his face. How much quiet did it take to read a paper, anyway?

She opened the book again. There had been something about "life's night" that reminded her of what Doug had been saying about extinction. There it was:

> Life's night begins; let him never come back to us!
> There would be doubt, hesitation and pain,
> Forced praise on our part—the glimmer of twilight,
> Never glad confident morning again!

Maybe there was a connection after all. If people lost faith in her father, it could be like that. It could be they would never trust him again. She wished she hadn't looked up the poem. Her father was right—it was better not to know what people were saying. Could anyone really believe that her father had committed any kind of "wrong to man"?

She closed the book again and glanced over at her table mate, only to find herself looking into her father's face on the front page. She stood up slowly, picked up the book, and slammed it down on the table as hard as she could. Without waiting for a response, she walked out of the library, down the front steps, and into the parking lot. As she climbed into the stifling car, squinting against the glare of the sun on its hood, she knew she wanted to go down to the Peg. She could find Doug and they could at least air the boat out, even if the water was still too high for going out on the river. If Doug was with her, and if they happened to see Joe, it wouldn't seem as if she'd planned it. She hoped Doug would be home.

When she drove up the driveway, Amanda saw that her mother's car was gone. That was probably a good sign. At least she had gone out somewhere, perhaps to play tennis. In the kitchen, Amanda checked to see if her mother had left a note, but didn't find one. The dishes were done. Maybe cleaning up the kitchen was a safety valve too.

She called for Doug, but he wasn't home yet. When she thought of going down to the marina alone, she changed her mind. Anyway, the sun was hot, the Peg would be dreadful, just sitting there in the marina without the river breeze. At least the house was cool. She went into the living room and fingered her way through the records. Debussy would be good, she thought—soothing, removed from the real world. As the music began, she sank onto the rose velvet sofa and kicked off her sandals. This whole room, with its white walls and white marble fireplace, the paintings, the piano, the shelves with her mother's porcelain collection, was *all* removed from the real world. When they were little, neither she nor Doug had been allowed in this room except on special occasions. Children didn't play on a rose beige carpet. Amanda sank deeper into the couch, resting her head on the thick back cushion.

Did they all run away? she wondered. She knew she did. But maybe Doug did too. Maybe his not having friends his own age was a kind of running. Instead of handling his differences, he just seemed to accentuate them and keep to himself. And her mother, always working for some good cause that had something to do with the "real" world. Did she ever really enter that world? How could she, in her linen suits and silk blouses and high heels. Or her tennis outfits. Maybe what her mother did was her way of building a barricade against whatever might be out there.

The world Joe had told her about, where girls got married and had kids by the time they were seventeen—she'd always known that world existed, but not for her. What would it be like to have a mother who stood all day behind a cash register and had never even owned a tennis dress? What would it be like, when the summer got hot and unbearable, to have to work all day on boat engines instead of taking the boats out and waterskiing? Julie was working

129

this summer, of course, but not because she needed the money. She had just wanted to try something different.

We *are* rich, she thought. She suspected there were no rooms in Joe's parents' house that didn't get used. She'd always loved this house, and her turret window with its view of the river. But she'd been aware always of the blowing of fuses and the warping of floorboards, of the windows that stuck and the basement that flooded. So it hadn't seemed all that special. Her friends lived in houses like it. She hadn't ever thought to compare it to the tiny tract houses north of town, or the narrow, dirty-looking row houses downtown, except to wonder how anyone could live like that. As if they lived there by choice.

She was just coming to the question of having three cars in one family, of her own white 280ZX, when the back door slammed. "Doug?" she called. "Is that you?"

"Yeah, it's me."

His voice sounded funny. Thick and muffled. She pushed herself up and went out into the kitchen. The water was running, and he was leaning against the sink. "What's wrong?" she asked. When he turned to face her, she gasped. Dried blood crusted his nose, his face was dirty and streaked with tears, and over one eye there was a huge, bluish lump. His clothes were muddy, and a ragged hole in the knee of his jeans showed a wide, bloody scrape. "What happened to you?"

"All-boy adventure," he said, his voice struggling for his usual joking tone. But he couldn't quite get it. Amanda hurried to him and put her arms around him. He burst into tears. She stood then, cradling his head while he sobbed.

"Does it hurt that bad?" she asked. He shook his head, but his sobs didn't stop. He sounded so utterly miserable, so desolate, that Amanda had to fight to keep herself from crying with him.

At last he began to quiet a little, gulping and sniffling. She pulled a paper towel off the rack over his head and handed it to him. He held it to his nose while she wet the dishcloth in the cold water that was still running. "Here. Clean yourself up with this, and I'll fix you an ice pack for that lump."

While he wiped gingerly at his face, she filled a plastic bag with ice cubes, wrapped it in a towel, then sat him down and handed him the ice pack. "You want to tell me what happened? Did you tangle with a freight train or what?"

Doug smiled carefully, and she saw that his lip was split in one corner. "A couple of guys jumped me."

"Jumped you? You mean they started beating up on you? For no reason?"

"Oh, they had a reason. Avenging the town's honor or something like that. They didn't have the vocabulary to express it very clearly."

"Who was it?"

"Just some guys. Gary Wilcox and his gang. Sixth graders with some kind of Incredible Hulk fixation."

"What did you do?"

"Fell down a lot." Doug took the ice pack away. "Mandy, this hurts worse than doing nothing."

"Keep it on. Maybe we can get the swelling down a little. Did you fight back?"

"Sure. It was a big mistake, though. I gave Gary a bloody nose too, and all it did was make him mad." Doug put the ice pack gently back against his forehead. "I liked it better when they were just righteously indignant. Mad, they get *really* mean!"

"How'd you get away?"

"Have you met that new guy at the marina? Joe Schmidt?" Amanda nodded. "Well, I'd been talking to

131

him about my river-level project just before that. He must have heard the yelling. He dragged the other guys off me and gave Wilcox one mean kick in the pants. He offered to borrow a car and bring me home, but I decided to walk. I thought my knee might get stiff on me if I didn't use it."

"You should have taken the ride. What if those kids had been waiting for you somewhere else?"

"Oh, I didn't think I needed to worry about that. The kick Joe gave Gary was enough to send him home, too. Anyway, I don't think they'd risk getting Joe after them again. For a kind of skinny guy, he's strong."

"Is your mouth all right? No loose teeth or anything?"

Doug shook his head. "I checked them all. Mandy, do you understand why those kids would do what they did? I mean, even if Dad did what people say he did, what's the point of beating me up?"

"No point, Doug. That's the trouble with you. You want there to be a reason for everything. A rational reason. There isn't always anything rational about the way people act. You want a cup of tea or cocoa or something?"

Doug shook his head. "Too hot. Iced tea, maybe. With lots of sugar and no lemon. The lemon would kill my lip!"

"Listen, Doug. Maybe some of what happened was about Dad. What happens to him happens to us too, sort of. But those guys were just using it as an excuse. Kids hate people who are different. Especially when they think the differences are somehow 'better.' "

"I don't think I'm better than they are."

"You don't have to. They think that. I guess it scares them when they see you don't care about being like them. As if they aren't good enough. So when they figured they had an excuse, they used it."

"I don't even understand why the indictment gave them the excuse."

Amanda dropped ice cubes into a glass. "None of it makes sense. My friends give me a party because they think Dad's guilty. Those women's groups cancel Mom because they think Dad's guilty. And those kids beat you up. The truth doesn't even seem to matter."

She poured tea over the ice and stirred in a huge spoonful of sugar. "Now, take this and a granola bar or something and go upstairs. Settle yourself on your bed and do something worthless. Watch television. Or read a comic book. You do *have* a comic book?"

"Somewhere. I'm not a freak."

"Okay. Read it. Or watch the tube. I suppose you wouldn't consider taking a nap."

"I haven't since I was three."

"You haven't been beaten to a pulp before, either. Never mind. Just go rest." She smoothed the hair away from his face. "Don't worry about irrational people. There's nothing you can do about them. And don't worry about us either. We're going to be all right." He left the kitchen, holding his tea and granola bars, limping slightly. "Put something on that knee," she called after him. "Wash it first."

When he was gone, she sat down at the table with her own glass of tea. She wished she could talk to someone, preferably her father. But she didn't like to call him during the working day, and she didn't want him to worry about Doug, either. She didn't know where her mother was. If she couldn't talk to anyone, she wanted to do something. She wanted to go find the kids who had jumped Doug and do something terrible to them. Joe's kick didn't seem like enough.

Joe. She could talk to Joe. She went into the living room, picked up her sandals, and took the record off. Obviously, a velvet sofa, rose beige carpet, and Debussy couldn't keep the real world out. Nothing could. At the bottom of the stairs, she called up to Doug. "I'm going out for a little—down to the marina. Will you be okay?"

"I'm fine," he called back.

"You want something else to eat?"

"Maybe later. Go ahead."

When she started the car, Amanda felt like crying. Or screaming. Or strangling those kids. People who care about the world are crazy, she thought. Or fools.

·11·

"I'd begun to think you'd disappeared off the face of the earth," Joe said, when Amanda finally found him, working in the marina's boat shed.

"I could say the same for you," she replied.

Joe wiped his hands on a rag and came over to her. "Did Doug get home okay? How's he doing?"

"He got home, and I guess he's all right. You could have called, you know."

"He didn't want me to do anything else. Sometimes you have to let kids handle things on their own—as much as possible."

"I didn't even know you two knew each other."

"My aunt introduced us a couple of days ago. She wanted me to meet somebody smarter than me."

"Can you get away from here for a few minutes—now?"

"Sure." Joe held the door for her and they went outside. "You want to walk or go up to the coffee shop or what?"

"Let's just walk."

"Right. If we walk toward your boat, nobody will have to wonder what we're doing together."

"I suppose you're protecting my image."

"Actually, I was thinking of my own."

Amanda stopped and Joe kept walking, then turned

back to her. He was grinning. "I have an awful time deciding when you're joking," she said.

"That's because I'm so deep. Come on. Let's go look at your boat."

The afternoon sun beat down on them and shimmered on the gravel of the marina's parking lot. Southern Ohio June had settled in with a vengeance.

"What's up?" Joe asked when they'd reached the gangway down to the docks.

"Nothing, really. I just needed to talk to somebody."

"About Doug? Don't let what those little creeps did get you down. He was terrific! When I got there, he was going after the biggest one on his knees, he was so mad. They kept knocking him down and he was crying, but he didn't run."

"Why do they do that? What do they get out of ganging up on a kid that way?"

Joe shook his head. "I don't know. But it must be something universal, because it happens everywhere. Especially to kids who are different. I ought to know." He made a muscle. "See that? I had to work out when I was little so I could get strong enough to handle the guys in my neighborhood."

"That doesn't seem right. I mean, why should a kid who doesn't want to fight in the first place have to learn how just to survive?"

"You've heard of survival of the fittest."

"When will 'fittest' mean something besides the one with the biggest muscles? Or the biggest gang?"

"Good question. It'll probably take a few million more years of evolution. If we have that long."

"You sound like Doug."

Joe laughed. "We have some things in common, Doug and I."

"You don't mind that he's rich?"

"He doesn't drive a fancy car!"

They laughed together, and Amanda wondered why she had ever thought his eyes could be menacing. In fact, they had the same depth and sparkle she had noticed in Doug's or in her father's, except that Joe's were so much darker. They had reached the slip where the Peg was tied. The water level had dropped, leaving the grass gray with dried mud. The surface of the creek was still coated with slime and debris.

"I told Doug that those kids are probably threatened by his being different from them. Do you suppose that's always true? Are people so insecure that they want to bring down anyone who's different?"

"That's why we're all so careful to look as if we belong. That's why I wear my hair the way I do and why you wear those alligators. I read once that if you paint a bird to look different from its flock and then release it among them, they'll peck it to death. At least it isn't just people."

Amanda shuddered. Did everyone do what she'd accused her mother of doing? Then what was the difference? "But if all we're doing is putting on an image people can judge on the outside, how does anybody ever know the truth about anybody else? Under the disguise?"

"Maybe they don't." Joe had never thought about it that way before. Was that true, he wondered? "Or maybe that's what love is for."

Amanda considered that. It felt right. That's how she knew her father, aside from the image he worked for. And maybe that's what was missing with her mother. "My father isn't fighting back the way Doug did," she said.

"Doug didn't *win* that way," Joe reminded her. "I had to help him."

"You think Dad needs somebody to help him, too?"

137

Joe kicked at a nail that was sticking up from the silvery-gray board near the edge of the dock. He had to be careful on this subject. "I would imagine he's fighting a different way. And he's been around long enough that you can bet he has help."

Amanda looked at the Peg, gleaming in the sun. There was a little scum around her hull at the waterline, but that was all. "Maybe we'll be like the boat," she said. "She didn't get all covered with mud like the grass. She rode out the flood, and its only everything else that's slimy."

"Maybe that's what your father is counting on. The way a boat survives is to stay above the flood." He wiped the sweat from his forehead. "It is really hot all of a sudden. And muggy. Is it always this way here in the summer?"

Amanda grinned, "Of course. It's a river valley. I keep thinking how good it will be to get out on the boat. It's the only way to survive the summer." When she'd said it, she realized how it must have sounded to him.

"Is that called survival of the richest?"

This time, she recognized the slight twist of his mouth. "Right. The richest and their friends. You want to come along when I take her out?"

"As long as you wait another day or two. The dams are still open and the current out there is pretty bad. To say nothing of the junk floating around. How good a pilot are you?"

"Terrific, of course. It's in the genes."

"Good. My genes are definite landlubbers."

"It's a date, then. The first day we can get out."

Joe touched her hand. "Never let it be said that differences deter *us*."

"I should probably get back," Amanda said. "I hate to leave Doug alone for too long."

"I'm sorry it took this thing with Doug to bring you down here, but I'm glad you came."

"Me too."

Joe glanced around, then took both of her hands in his. "Try not to take the way people are reacting to all this too seriously. Remember the Peg. Just try to ride it out."

"As long as somebody doesn't try to give me a bloody nose."

"If they do, just remember I'm here."

When she got home, Amanda was surprised to see that her father's car was there. Apparently her mother still wasn't home.

She pulled her car into its space, climbed out and stood for a moment in the dim, stuffy interior of the old carriage house. Her father's dark BMW gleamed quietly; someone on his staff kept it washed and waxed. Standing there between her father's car and her own, with the empty, shadowed space where her mother's compact station wagon wasn't, Amanda thought again about Joe's definition of rich. If three cars in the family didn't necessarily mean vast wealth, it certainly wasn't poverty, either. As she came out into the sun again and started toward the house, she noticed the little stirrup on her Aigner sandals. Another sign of belonging, or a way to shut others out, or both?

As she closed the back door, grateful to be in the cool house, her father came into the kitchen, his tie pulled down, his shirt sleeves rolled up. He held his arms out to her, and she ran into them, hugging him hard. They stayed there for a moment, then he kissed her forehead. "I'm glad to see you don't have a black eye or a bloody nose or anything. I suppose your friends have abandoned you."

"Nope. I've abandoned them."

"That's one way to handle it. Maybe not the best."

Amanda hugged him tighter. "Don't worry about me."

"All right." He gently took her arms from around his waist and held her hands. Amanda noticed that the creases in his face, the shadows under his eyes, seemed deeper than ever. He looked tired. "I just told Doug, but I don't want either of you to get worried about this. Your mother went to Aunt Gail's for a few days."

"Aunt Gail's? Mom went to Michigan without even saying anything?"

"She called me before she left." He released her hands and leaned against the counter, too elaborately casual. "She just went up for a visit. She'll be back the first of next week. She wanted to get away for a little."

"Who from?"

"Just away. Don't start judging, Mandy. She thought she'd be able to sort things out a little better away from the publicity."

It must be nice, Amanda thought. None of the rest of them could do that. But she didn't say it.

"What kind of food do you want to have for dinner? I thought I'd get something out."

"You don't have to do that," Amanda said. "I'll fix something. Why don't you go rest."

He ran his hand through his hair. "Actually, there are a few things I ought to do before dinner. I'll be in the den. You're sure you don't mind?"

"No problem. Are you in any hurry? There isn't anything thawed."

"No hurry. But you'd better check with Doug."

"I'll take him another snack. Did you talk to him?"

"A little. He's got a dilly of an eye." James Sterling hurried toward the den, obviously unwilling to talk more

140

about Doug. He probably feels responsible, Amanda thought, as she took a package of frozen hamburger from the freezer.

Half an hour later, Amanda left a kettle of sloppy Joes simmering on the stove and took Doug a chunk of cheese and some grapes. He was working on a model of a geodesic dome when she went into his room. His eye, still swollen, was now a livid purple. "It's okay, Mandy," Doug said, carefully fitting a strut into a plastic coupling. "It looks a lot worse than it feels by now."

"I told you to rot your mind."

Doug grinned up at her. "My mind refused to be rotted. What can I do? Anyway, the dome's good therapy."

"What did Dad have to say about the fight?"

"Not much. He said he hoped I'd given as good as I got. I think he felt worse about it than he wanted to let on."

"Probably."

"I was glad. If he'd been very sympathetic, I might have cried again."

"He says he told you about Mom."

"Yeah." Doug looked at her thoughtfully. "I suppose you're mad at her, huh?"

"Well, aren't you? It's a rotten time to jump ship, don't you think?"

He shrugged. "It depends. She isn't deserting. Maybe she needs to get away a little to be sure she won't desert. She'll be back when she says she will be."

"I guess." Amanda started out into the hall, turned back at the door. "Don't you ever get mad at anybody?"

"I got mad at Gary Wilcox today." He blinked. "You see how much good it does to get mad!"

"You're unreal!" She closed his door, then remembered what she had come up for. "Dinner won't be ready for an hour and a half."

141

Doug's voice rose to a squeal. "Are you trying to starve me to death?"

"Eat your cheese!"

As she went down the stairs, Amanda thought that her mother's leaving had been an odd choice for a person so concerned with her image. She had to know that it would look worse if people thought she'd left because of the indictment. It certainly didn't help.

As she passed the open door of the den, she saw her father at his desk, his head in his hands. He looked terribly alone. She knocked on the doorframe. "Can I come in, Dad?"

He looked up, shuffled a few papers, and nodded. "Sure, honey."

"I just felt like talking a little." She sat on the love seat that faced the desk. "Doug doesn't blame you for that fight, you know."

"I know." Her father stared over her head out the window, shaded from the afternoon sun by a huge honeysuckle outside. "There are things you can't help in this business. But it's no fun to come home and see your son with an eye like that." He lowered his gaze and looked at her. "And it's no fun to see your daughter avoiding her friends, or your wife having to leave town, even for a few days. Still, that's a chance you take."

Amanda looked away from her father's drawn face and noticed the long scratch that ran across the front of the desk. She had made that scratch when she was eight. The desk had been the back wall of a tent she'd made one day when she was playing Indian. Chased by an enemy tribe, she had dived for safety in her tent, carrying the curtain rod she'd been using for a spear. She'd thwarted her enemies, but her spear had gouged the desk from one side to the other. Knowing how furious her mother would be when she found it, Amanda had stayed inside the tent all afternoon, hiding, trying to figure out some way of covering up the evidence. She had just about decided to try coloring the scratch with brown crayon when her father had come home and entered her tent on his hands and knees to greet her. He'd discovered the catastrophe of course, and had promised to handle her mother.

"It's only a piece of furniture, Peg," he'd said, when her mother had been as angry as Amanda expected. "It isn't 'worthy of love.' She is!" Until that day, Amanda hadn't known that a name, like any other word, could have a meaning. It had changed her whole sense of herself for a while. Even now, all these years later, that scratch carried with it multiple associations. One was the memory of that paralyzing fear when she'd seen what she'd done. Another was the security of her father's protection, the comfort of his easy forgiveness, of his love. And there was pride, too, in the name her parents had chosen for her.

"Amanda?" her father said, and she looked up with a start.

"I'm sorry, Dad. I was just thinking about the scratch."

"Scratch?"

"Don't you remember? That scratch I made on your desk with the curtain rod."

"Oh. Yes."

But she knew he didn't remember. After all, it couldn't have been very important to him. How could he know how much it had meant to her? "I was just thinking how this house and the furniture sort of tell the story of our family. You know, there's the place on the dining room table where Doug's model glue took all the finish off. And the chip in the kitchen sink enamel where Mom dropped the cast-iron frying pan that time she picked it up without a hot pad. And the front steps we had to have poured all over again when you tried to do them yourself."

Her father frowned. "Can't we think of something else for me? I prefer the bookshelves I put in the upstairs hall—entirely by myself."

She grinned. "I'll settle for that. And there's the growth door in your bedroom, with that scratch you put on it way down by the floor when Doug first came home from the hospital. Remember, you laid him on the floor and marked how high his head came?"

"That I remember! We've had a good life here, haven't we?"

"Sure. Even if we do trip over the floors in the summer."

"Ah," he wagged his finger at her. "But in the summer, there's the Peg. She more than makes up for bumpy floors. We've had some good times on the river."

"I'll say." They sat for a moment, not speaking. Amanda thought of the rows of photo albums on the shelves behind her father's desk. Peg Sterling had carefully arranged the pictures in them, complete with captions, one album for every year they'd been married. Amanda had always loved to look at them. Would there be photographs for an album this summer? "Dad? Are you sure Mom isn't right that you ought to deny the charges in that indictment? People believe in you. If you just came out and told them that you didn't take a bribe, they'd accept that. They'd have to know you weren't lying."

Her father sighed. "I remember what it's like to be sixteen, Amanda. Everything seems either black or white. And most people seem to be honest and trusting and loyal. But that isn't the way things really are. The world is a great deal more complex than that. There isn't very much

144

black or white at all, just lots of shades of gray. And most of those are so close, you can't even tell them apart."

"I don't think I understand."

"The thing is, you can't just do 'good' things. It isn't possible. There are always people, sometimes very powerful people, who don't want those things to be done. So you have to find ways to do what you think should be done without getting stopped by them. Or crushed. When something good does get done, the people responsible can't always be too proud of what they had to do to make it possible."

"But—"

"Most people know that, or at least suspect it. So when a politician comes along telling everybody his hands are completely clean, it's hard to believe him. A man can open his mouth and say any words he wants to say. But you know the expression, 'Talk's cheap.' Why would anyone believe me?"

Amanda stood up. For some reason, she found it hard just to sit there and listen. "They'd believe you because they know you're a good mayor. And a good person."

James Sterling picked up a pen and moved it back and forth between his hands. "Maybe having been a good mayor isn't the best recommendation. They know I've managed to get a lot of things for this town. Maybe they don't think I could have done that without getting my hands a little dirty."

The room seemed suddenly stifling, as if the air conditioner had quit. "But if they think politicians are crooked, and if a good politician is especially crooked, why would they make such a big fuss over all this in the first place?"

"Because most of the time people don't have to confront what they know about how things get done. They can vote for somebody who's advertised as a 'Sterling character' and feel good about it. Then, if everything goes well, they can sit back and congratulate themselves for their wise choice. But if somebody starts talking about *how* things are going so well, they have to raise a great hue and cry. They can't admit to themselves that they'd tolerate dishonesty just to get done what they want done."

Amanda stared at the scratch on the desk. But there was no comfort in it now, no associations at all. It was just a scar in the gleaming surface of the wood. "What are you trying to tell me?"

"That I work in a world with no blacks and whites, Amanda. None."

She looked at him now. He was regarding her steadily. For some reason, his face seemed suddenly unfamiliar. As if he were staring out at her from the pages of a magazine. Someone she'd never seen before. She opened her mouth, but couldn't bring herself to ask what she wanted to ask. The air between them seemed to be filling up with seconds, ticking away in hot heavy silence. "Are you saying you took that bribe?" she asked finally.

He didn't answer immediately. She had the feeling that he'd gone out from behind his eyes. " 'Bribe' is a very particular word, Mandy. It means a reward for doing something wrong, something that you wouldn't do otherwise."

"You know what I mean."

"I recommended Dyer's company for exactly the reasons I said I did. It was time to break the impasse and we needed to keep the jobs in town."

"You didn't answer my question. Did you take the money?"

James Sterling set the pen down very carefully on the desk blotter in front of him, as if he were afraid it would break. "You can't know the future, Amanda. I didn't know

146

Charlie Dyer would cut corners. And I didn't know whether one of the other companies that bid on the gym would cut corners. Anyone might have. I *did* know it would be good for Grantsport for a local company to get that contract."

Amanda stared at the painting on the wall behind her father. It was a square rigged ship sailing through huge waves, the foam spraying out from its prow, heavy clouds churning across the sky. Her voice came out in a bare whisper. "You shouldn't have taken money."

Her father stared at the pen in front of him. "No. I shouldn't have taken money."

Amanda turned away, looking out the window. Her eyes burned, her heart was racing. She took a deep breath. This was her father, she told herself firmly. He hadn't changed. Less than an hour ago, when they had stood together in the kitchen, hugging each other, she had taken comfort from him, from his strength and his love. Only minutes ago, she had thought how alone he looked. It was what had brought her in here. But none of that seemed to make any difference. Something fundamental had changed. Something that could never be changed back. She turned back to him. "You're wrong about blacks and whites. Taking money is black. That's not gray! That's black!"

She was in the hallway almost before she knew she had moved. She plunged on through the kitchen and out onto the flagstone path in the backyard, gasping as she hit what felt like a wall of heat, like a steaming sponge. When she reached the garage, she stopped. Her Datsun hadn't changed either. But she couldn't bring herself to touch it. Her father had given her that car for her birthday. How much of the money he had taken had helped pay for her car? She had never asked herself where the money came from that paid for their house, the Peg, everything else. It had just been there. Did her parents have money from

147

their families? She had no idea. She remembered Steve's words. The governorship doesn't come cheap.

A sharp pain struck between her eyes. There had been no lead-up, just this sudden, clutching pain. She turned, gingerly, trying to avoid jolting her head. Already, the edges of objects were beginning to blur. The hedge along the driveway was scarcely more than a dark green shadow. She seemed able to focus only in the center, on a strip of pavement, oil-stained and pitted, down the driveway. Without consciously making a decision, she started down the drive, walking quickly, finally breaking into a run, pain lancing through her head with every step. At the bottom she turned toward the marina.

·12·

Though there were a few people at the marina making last-minute preparations for the beginning of the delayed season, Amanda paid no attention to any of them. A man who was mopping the deck of his houseboat two slips down waved, but Amanda didn't wave back. She just began taking the Peg's canvas off, yanking at the snaps, trying to concentrate on her hands through the haze of her headache. When she'd loosened the canvas she could reach from the dock, she stepped into the boat and began to work on the side next to the water. She was reaching to get the last of the snaps on the cabin roof, when Doug's voice, calling her name, startled her. She turned to see him coming down the dock, breathing hard, one hand pressed to his side. "What are you doing?" he asked.

"What does it look like?" She didn't want him there. She yanked loose the last bit of canvas.

"I've been trying to catch up with you," he said, bending over to catch his breath. "I heard."

She dropped the canvas at her feet. "What did you hear?"

"Just the end." His eyes filled with tears. "It was enough."

"You shouldn't have been listening."

"Does that matter?" He rubbed at his eyes, wincing as

149

he touched the swollen one. "He did what they say he did."

"Yes." She kicked at the mass of pale green canvas and wished Doug hadn't followed her. What comfort could she offer him, with a headache sending searing flashes through her temples? She had no comfort for him or for herself. "Well, don't just stand there. As long as you're here, you might as well help me fold this."

She heaved the mass of material out onto the dock. Together, they stretched it out and folded it. When it was reduced to a neat oblong, she took the key off the hook on the side of the console and sat on the leather-upholstered captain's chair.

"You aren't taking her out, are you?" Doug asked.

"Yes, I am." Amanda pushed the damp hair off her forehead. "You didn't think I came down here just to sit on her, did you? The sun'll be up for hours yet."

"But the river . . ." Doug started.

Amanda pulled out the choke, shoved the throttle ahead, and turned the key. She hoped the engine would start. It hadn't been run for weeks. "Listen, Doug. I'm going out. The water level has dropped enough for the big houseboats to get out under the bridge."

"Yes, but the current."

The engine turned over sluggishly and died. "Come on, come on," she breathed. "You can come with me if you want," she said to Doug, "or you can go back home. But I'm going. I have to get out on the river for a while!"

Doug stood for a moment, shifting his weight from foot to foot. Then he shrugged. "You ready to have her untied?"

"Wait till I get her started." Amanda tried again. Again the engine turned over and died. "You can do it, Peg," she said. This time, the engine caught and roared to life, coughing and sputtering, but gradually steadying. She pushed in the choke and eased the throttle back. The power of the engine throbbed under her. This is why I love the boat, she thought. "Bow first," she called to Doug.

"I know." He untied the bow line and coiled it neatly around the cleat on the dock. Then he untied the stern line from the cleat, keeping one hand on the boat. "Ready?"

Amanda revved the engine slightly. The smooth steady roar was what it should be. She checked the gauges. Everything was normal. "Check the exhaust."

"Water's coming out," Doug said.

"Okay. Jump on."

Doug pushed off from the dock and leaped over the transom as the Peg pulled into the channel. Amanda guided the boat steadily between the two rows of slips. The headache was still pounding against her skull, but her vision had cleared. In fact, the panorama of slips and boats in front of her seemed almost unnaturally defined. Almost as if each object had a line around it, like the black lines in a coloring book. She glanced up at the sky. Though the sun was still hot, the sky was a hazy, yellowish gray, the air still and heavy. She checked the gas gauge. More than three-quarters full. It was a good thing they didn't need gas. Even if someone happened to be at the gas dock, which wasn't likely, they'd probably try to keep her from going out. And if it were Joe—she pushed the thought of Joe out of her mind. What had she told him about her father? Something smug and complacent. It was too humiliating to think about.

Doug went down into the cabin, rummaged in the locker under the forward bunk, and came back, slipping his arms into his red nylon life jacket. Amanda glanced at him and looked away. His face bore not only the darkening purple, which had now spread to surround his eye completely, but another kind of pain as well.

151

She breathed deeply, taking in the heavy smell of mud and fish, savoring even the thickness of the humid air. The wheel under her hands felt the same, as did the vibration of the engine and its deep, pulsing throb. She felt her heart, which had been racing ever since she'd left the house, begin to slow down to its normal pace. Whatever had brought her to the river had been right. Like an instinct. Like whatever made baby sea turtles struggle across a beach they'd never seen to reach the ocean. As the gas dock slipped by on her left, and the huge, ancient, stone bridge loomed ahead, she could feel the headache beginning to loosen its hold, retreating ever so slowly, as it sometimes did when she'd taken one of the pills the doctor had prescribed.

Doug stood on the port side, watching the bank move steadily by, the weeds and poison ivy gray with dried mud. Amanda hadn't wanted Doug to come with her. She had wanted to get off by herself, to try to make some sense out of the impossibility she knew, now, to be true. But she was glad that he was here. Maybe being on the river could do for him what she knew it would do for her. Maybe together they could move fast enough to blow the pain away.

As the shadow of the bridge fell across them, Doug looked up at the underside, watching the water that perpetually dripped from the mossy stone. Amanda had an impulse, as they passed under it, to honk the horn. It was always startling, echoing back at them from the granite of the bridge. But that was her father's trick. He would do it every time, knowing they knew he was going to, knowing that even so, they would jump. A few drops fell on the canopy above her, and they came out from under the bridge. Doug glanced at her as if he, too, had thought of the horn. Then he looked back at the bank. Most of her life, Amanda thought, she had been unable to feel about

Doug the way a big sister should feel. Six years older than he, she had found herself almost looking up to him as if he were the older one. He had always seemed so together, so sure of himself. It was as if he had anchored himself to the earth, to its millions of years of history, its evolution, its solid rock. Now, it seemed, even that anchor wouldn't hold. He was, after all, a ten-year-old boy who could be beaten up by other boys, who could cry, and who could follow his sister, not to keep her from one of her foolish whims but to be with her, no matter what she was doing. And he was standing there now, watching the water flow under the boat, trusting her to handle whatever came along. At this moment, they had only each other. And neither would let the other down.

They had nearly reached the mouth of the creek. Ahead of them, the water changed from the smooth, quiet water of the creek to a rush of brown, churning past the points of land on either side. As the Peg's bow moved beyond the fishing point, Amanda saw the crates stacked up again, beside the trees. Only a few nights ago she and Joe had sat there in the light from his lantern. And she had said—she remembered it now, too clearly—she had said that her father was good. As simple as that. She turned the boat with the current and pushed it up to cruising speed. The bow lifted, and they headed downriver.

Joe put the engine cover back down and stood up, circling his head on his neck to relieve the tension in his shoulders from bending over his work. By tomorrow, or the next day more likely, everyone would be wanting boats ready for the river. This was the third engine he had tuned that day, and he was ready for supper. The heat was awful, but at least the sun wasn't beating down the way it had been earlier in the day. Breathing in this air is like breath-

153

ing in a steam bath, he thought. The houseboat was air-conditioned, and he looked forward to the evening, when he could work on the story that was growing out of the character sketch he had begun. Aunt Myra and Uncle Frank had probably already left for Cincinnati, for the Reds game, but his supper was supposed to be waiting for him at the coffee shop, where he could warm it up in the microwave before taking it back to the boat. A whole evening alone, Joe thought. No television, no conversation, just the boat to himself.

As he walked up toward the coffee shop, he was surprised to hear a boat engine roar to life. There were people working on their boats, of course, but most of them were doing cleaning and external work. Maybe it was just someone trying out an engine, he decided, and would have dismissed it, except that the engine didn't stop as he'd expected it to. Instead, it settled into the heavy throb of idle speed. He went on to the coffee shop, which was on ground high enough to overlook the three channels of the marina and the creek as far as the gas dock.

The boat was the Peg o' My Heart, he saw immediately. Amanda was at the wheel, Doug was next to her, donning a life jacket. Surely, they weren't planning to go out on the river. A couple of people had tried it earlier, but had come back almost immediately. Between the current and the amount of junk in the water, they'd said it was crazy to be out. He remembered Amanda's promise to take him on the first trip, and her assurance that she was a good pilot. If she was so good, what was she doing risking a trip before the river was down? He thought of calling to her, but she'd never be able to hear him over the sound of the engine. And she was already too far to see him waving. He watched until the boat disappeared behind the trees and the ridge beyond the gas dock. He hoped she knew what she was doing. She'll be back when she sees what it's like out there, he assured himself.

He checked the sky. The murky haze had thickened in the last hour or two, but the sun was still high. Sunset was more than two hours away. He shrugged. No sense worrying about a river person. But he wished she had come looking for him. She had called it a date, the first trip.

When he had warmed his food and was heading back to the houseboat, Joe remembered what one of the men who'd gone out this afternoon had said: "It's the deadheads I don't like out there—I came on what I thought were some branches, and it turned out to be a huge, damn tree, so waterlogged the whole trunk was under. I swerved in time to miss it, but I came back in. I don't feel like having the bottom of my boat ripped out." Joe hoped Amanda would come back quickly.

In the houseboat, Joe settled himself at the big table in the galley and turned on the radio. The rock music was growing on him, he realized, as he dug into the plate of spaghetti in front of him. He was catching himself sometimes, moving with the beat. Maybe, when he went back to classical music, he'd find it dull, without that insistent beat to drag him along. Of course, it was only the body it dragged, not the mind.

Listening to rock music was part of belonging, too, he thought. Part of the uniform. And the beat made it easy to dance to, so that everybody could dance pretty much the same way. Amanda had called him a snob, and he'd had to admit that he was. But when they'd talked this afternoon, he'd begun to wonder if that wasn't the human condition. There were exceptions, of course, people like his Aunt Myra, who seemed really able to accept people for what they were, aside from the uniforms they wore. But most people judged everybody else by what was easiest to see.

155

He finished his supper and stacked the dishes in the sink, then went to his cabin to get his story. What he'd said to Amanda this afternoon—about love helping to get past differences—might be true. As his story had grown, he was beginning to care more about his characters, as if they were real. And the more he cared, the more he seemed to know how they must feel. He sat down, kicked off his thongs, and put his bare feet on the chair across the table. He needed to reread the story before he could begin. Maybe, with the whole evening to work, he could get it done tonight.

Out on the river, Amanda eased the throttle back. There was more debris than she'd ever seen before. Twice now, she'd had to swerve to avoid a log she'd barely seen until they were nearly on top of it. "Trashy out here," she called to Doug, who was hanging onto the rail on the port side.

"Will it be easier if we go slower?"

"Sure. I just need to see what's up there in time to avoid it."

"Where are we going?" he asked.

"Just downriver a way. I won't go too far, because it'll be harder going back upstream."

Doug nodded. His knuckles were white where he gripped the wood, but she thought he looked a little less miserable than when they'd left the marina.

"Come over here," she said, and held out one arm. After a moment, he went to stand next to her. She put her arm around his shoulder and squeezed. "You okay?" Doug nodded. "Me, too." She sighed. "I think."

"It's good to be out here," Doug said. "It sort of feels as if nothing has changed."

Amanda eased the wheel to the right. Something that looked like an old steamer trunk was floating up ahead. "Because this doesn't change. Oh, sometimes it's high and

156

sometimes it's rough, but it's always just the river." She pointed to the rusting hulk of an old barge against the bank, its stern underwater, its angled prow pointed upward toward the line of trees. A cream-and-coffee-colored foam swirled around it, and a tangle of branches had jammed against its upriver side. "Remember the time you caught a fish off that? Mom had called you to come back to the boat. She had just said there weren't any fish around there, and even if there were, you'd never catch one."

"And I pulled up a catfish big enough for dinner."

They both laughed. "She tried to save face by saying that you couldn't really call it a fish, since it didn't have any scales."

They went on cruising slowly, Amanda going carefully, staying far out from the bank, where she thought there would be less debris. She had never been out when the water was still so high, and the banks looked strange. Where the beaches usually were. the water was still up to the weeds, in among the willow scrub. If they wanted to tie up, it would be hard to know where the bottom was, or what might be just under the waterline.

"Is there anything to eat on board?" Doug asked.

"How should I know? Go see."

He came back grinning, with a handful of crackers. "Hurray for Tupperware," he said, and dumped them onto the console. "They aren't even bendy." He went back for more. "But there's no peanut butter."

"That's because it got so weird from the heat that Mom decided not to leave it on board. If you wanted peanut butter, you should have brought it."

Doug laughed. It was a family saying that got a constant workout on the boat. "If you wanted Scrabble, you should have brought it," he said.

"If you wanted Coke . . ." Amanda added.

"If you wanted an anchor." They laughed again. Once, when James Sterling had decided to rearrange the stowing of their gear, they had actually gone off, leaving both the stern and the bow anchors lying on the dock. It had been Doug, age seven, who had said it that time.

Amanda rubbed her forehead and pushed her hair back. The headache had gone. And Doug was laughing. They'd have to start back soon, she knew, but it was good just to be together and to feel the air against their faces and the movement of the boat underfoot.

"That's the last of them," Doug said around a mouthful of cracker. He looked up at the sky. "Mandy, are those clouds over us now? Or is the sun just going down?"

Amanda looked up. The sun was lower, but had faded to a faint, yellowish disk behind the dirty white of the sky. The haze was thickening, certainly. She pulled the throttle back and the Peg slowed, rising and then falling in the surge of her own wake coming under her stern. The air was hot, still, even heavier than it had been.

"I don't like the feel of it," Doug said. "Let's go back."

Amanda looked at the sun again, ahead of them, just over the Kentucky hills. What had been a pale disk was now nothing but a brighter patch in the haze, and even as she watched, it began to fade out entirely. Ahead, where the river curved out of sight, there was a greenish tinge to the fast-darkening haze. She felt the hair rise along her arms. The leaves of the trees along the bank hung suspended, totally still. Amanda tried to make her voice light. "You're probably right. No sense being out if it's going to rain." As she turned the boat, hoping Doug hadn't noticed the color of the sky ahead, Amanda cursed herself. It had never even occurred to her to check the weather forecast before they left. After all that rain, she hadn't even considered the possibility of a storm. She knew better. It was the first rule she'd ever learned about boating. Particularly for this time of year. She pushed the throttle forward again. The Peg was making slow progress; the current was faster than she'd realized. And they were farther downriver than she'd thought, too. She wished she hadn't seen that color. It was June, not too late for tornados. Any other time, she'd have noticed the oppressive heat that had been building all afternoon. That muggy stillness alone would have kept her off the river. But she hadn't thought about it. She smacked her fist against the chart book on the console. She hadn't even turned on the weather-band radio.

"Do you think we can outrun it?" Doug asked.

So he did know. "I hope so. We wouldn't be able to make much speed against this current, even if we didn't have to watch out for deadheads."

"Can I do anything?"

Amanda resisted the urge to look over her shoulder. She knew that if she saw that line of darkness approaching, she might panic. The thing to do now was to keep her head. "Go open the hatch and keep a lookout from up there. Point if you see anything I need to steer around. Maybe we can go faster that way."

Doug nodded and went back down into the cabin. Moments later, the hatch slid back in its tracks and Doug's head and shoulders appeared. Amanda became aware of a low rumbling. Every so often there was a louder, sharper crash, but mostly the sound was continuous. Like a dog, growling in its sleep. It was getting louder. Amanda tried to remember how fast a storm front could move. Hadn't she heard weather forecasters say forty miles an hour? Could that be right? If so, there was no way they were going to be able to outrun it. Even on a calm day going with the current, the Peg couldn't make that speed.

"Deadhead!" Doug yelled. "Starboard!" She steered

slightly left, away from the direction he was pointing. The sky was getting dark so fast now that she could see the change in the shade of the greens along the bank. The leaves were still hanging limp. The air seemed almost too thick to breathe.

A flash, gone almost before she had seen it, lighted the Peg for a moment, and she counted under her breath. "One, two, three," and the crash came, seeming to split the air. The storm wasn't on them yet, but they couldn't possibly get back to the marina. Maybe they could get to Brown's Creek. They could find some shelter there. If the storm hit while they were in the middle of the river—she groaned. During the only storms she had ever been through on the Peg her father had taken care of everything, and they had always managed to tie up safely before a storm actually hit.

"Something to port!" Doug shouted. "And it's getting so dark I can hardly see!"

A splash landed on the windshield in front of her. Then another and another. The rain had come, and the wind would come now too. There was no time to get to Brown's Creek. "Close the hatch!" she yelled.

Doug came scrambling back to the wheel. "We'd better make for the bank," he said. The rain was coming steadily now, blurring the windshield.

"Get into the cabin," Amanda said. "And throw me a life jacket!" Why did she never bother with a life jacket? She turned toward the bank, looking for an open stretch. Everywhere, the willow scrub seemed to reach out into the water. The rain was coming hard and fast now, blowing in on her. The trees tossed violently in the wind. The Peg rose and fell on the heavy chop that had kicked up as the wind swept along the water against the current.

She spotted an open spot on the bank—it would be a

beach when the water was lower—and eased back on the throttle. She was afraid of going in too fast, unable to see what might be between her and the bank. But just as the Peg slowed, she realized the mistake. She had angled too sharply and, with less power, she had lost crucial control. The Peg wallowed between two waves, rolling heavily. Shoving the throttle, she corrected her course, easing off on the angle, but now having to head for the bank where the scrub was thick.

Doug was beside her, wiping the rain from his eyes, holding out a life jacket. "I can't put it on now," she said. "Hang it on my seat."

"You want me to get the anchor?"

"No!" she shouted. Even standing together, it was hard to hear each other over the rising roar of the wind and the lashing of the rain. "I'm going to ground her and then try to get her tied to a tree. Just get me some rope."

With an ear-shattering crash, lightning struck the hillside across the river. At least the hills on both sides were high, Amanda thought, and the lightning would strike there instead of into the water. Just then another bolt crashed deafeningly into the trees on the Ohio side. The rain was lashing directly against the windshield now, the wind coming across the starboard bow as she tried to keep the boat pointed toward the bank. How can that be? The storm is moving upriver, but the wind is coming downriver, Amanda thought. "Get inside!" she screamed at Doug, as lightning flashed again and the thunder crashed so violently that she ducked, as if avoiding a blow. The Peg was pitching now, lashed by wind that seemed to be coming from every direction at once. Amanda pushed the throttle as far as it would go, threw her weight against it, and headed for the bank, which had to be close now but was almost invisible in the darkness behind a wall of rain.

Instead of the reassuring thud of the bow running up onto the mud, there was a splintering crash, and the boat rose under her feet. She was thrown sideways, her head crashing into the bulkhead. She fell to her knees, and shook her head to clear it. She tried to stand, slipped on the wet wood, and grabbed for the captain's chair. She pulled herself up to the wheel, the Peg rearing and bucking, out of control in the maelstrom of waves and wind. She ducked as the thunder crashed. Which way was the bank? She had lost her bearings. The crash must have been the Peg hitting something—something that had torn a hole in her bow. "Doug!" she screamed. The wheel turned, jerking itself out of her hands. "Doug! Where are you?"

There was no answer. She grabbed at the wheel, but just as she felt her hands close on it, the Peg was lifted again, and heeled over to port. With a great rush, the boat was thrust sideways and came to a sickening, thudding stop against the bank. The impact threw Amanda down again, and a pain shot through her wrist and up her arm to the shoulder.

Lightning and thunder were continuous now, and she could barely see in the sudden, blinding flashes, followed by dark purple and yellow afterimages. The Peg had been grounded almost on her side, but Amanda felt the continuous movement as waves buffeted her. The power that had thrust her ashore could pull her off again, she thought. "Doug!" she called again, fighting down the panic that was rising in her chest. From the rope locker under the wheel she took the heaviest rope she could find and scrambled over the side onto the mud. The rain was coming so hard that she couldn't even breathe facing into the wind. It was like being underwater. Turning her back against the wind, she struggled to the bow and got a loop of rope through and around a cleat. Then she fought her way up

162

the bank through the willows that slapped her across the face and chest. There was nothing big enough to tie the Peg to, but there had to be bigger trees farther up the bank. She hoped the rope was long enough. Finally, she tripped on the exposed roots of an enormous, split-trunked willow. She wrapped the line around it, securing it as tightly as she could. Every movement of her left hand sent searing pains up her arm.

She wished she could stay there, in the shelter of the tree, where the wind and rain were not so violent. But Doug was on the Peg. She hoped he had only been too frightened to answer her. Or that he hadn't heard her over the wind and thunder.

When she reached the Peg, the wind seemed to have slacked off a little. But the thunder and lightning were still raging, apparently directly on top of her. She wondered what would happen if lightning struck the river while she was standing in the water. When people talked about lightning and water, they only said, "Don't be on the water during a thunderstorm." She couldn't remember ever hearing what to do if you *were* on the water.

As she started to climb back into the Peg, she put her weight for a moment on her left hand, and the pain was like a fire in her arm. She dragged herself on board, using her right arm, trying to keep her left out of the way. She crawled, slipping against the angle of the boat, to the companionway, and pulled herself through and down the angled stairs. It was pitch dark inside, but in the flashes of lightning, she made out Doug's form. He was lying half on and half off the forward bunk, his head against the bulkhead.

"Doug?" He didn't move. The boat was still being jolted by the waves against her side. Amanda fell twice trying to get to him. But finally, she pulled herself to her knees next to him and reached out to touch his face. His cheek felt cold. She moved her hand to the hollow beneath his ear, and felt the steady pulse. As she breathed in, she discovered she'd been holding her breath. Carefully, she smoothed the hair away from his forehead, and gasped at the sticky warmth under her hand. His hair was covered with blood. "Please," she whispered. "Please let him be all right."

Amanda wanted to move him, to put him someplace more comfortable, but with the angle of the boat, there was nowhere. She was kneeling in water herself. Water. She felt along under the water till she found the splinters where whatever they'd hit had come through the hull. The hole wasn't big. If it had been, they'd have gone down, she thought. Even in this mess, perhaps they'd been lucky.

The jolting was less violent now. The sound of wind and rain was lessening too. She got herself up onto the tilted bunk next to Doug's head and braced herself against the hull. There was nothing she could do now except wait. Wait for the storm to blow itself out, and for someone to come looking for them. No one knew they'd come out onto the river, of course. But maybe someone had seen them leave the marina. By the time the storm was completely over, she realized, it could be dark. So it could be morning before anyone would come looking. She hoped someone would come soon. She had never felt so helpless and alone. Doug looked so small in his shorts and life jacket, his arms and legs so thin. She looked at his pale face, at the dark patch of blood in his hair, and realized that she could see him now. A pale gray light filtered down through the clear plastic of the hatch. The storm had moved on up the river. At least, if it's moving fast, she thought, it passes fast, too. She cradled her left wrist in her lap and settled in to wait.

·13·

"The National Weather Service has issued an advisory for the Ohio Valley," the voice was saying. Joe put down his pen. "A tornado watch is in effect from now until eleven P.M. While no tornadoes have been sighted, radar indicates a line of thundershowers, possibly severe, advancing toward Grantsport. Gale-force winds and damaging hail may accompany the storms. Listeners are advised to stay tuned for further bulletins."

Joe looked out the window. The sky was still light, but the haze had thickened. Had Amanda come back? He slipped his feet into his thongs and went out onto the deck. The air was hot, still, oppressive. He hurried toward the Sterling's slip, hoping to see the Peg tied safely, Amanda and Doug on her back deck. But long before he got there, he could see that the slip was empty. What could he do? It was possible that they'd heard the warning and tied up somewhere, maybe in one of the other creeks that emptied into the river. Probably they were as safe in the boat right now as they would be in the marina. He stared at the oblong of oily water where the boat should be. But what if they hadn't heard? What if they were out on the open river?

He wished he knew more about boats. He could go out

165

after them, but he'd be no better off out there than they would—worse. He'd driven the houseboat before, but only in the middle of the river. He'd never even brought the Marina Queen in to the gas dock. Handling a fifty-foot houseboat was not like driving a car. He'd have to find someone. His uncle would be on the road. James Sterling. Amanda's father would know what to do.

"On the river?" the mayor asked, when Joe had reached him and explained. "Are you sure?"

"I saw the Peg leaving the marina about an hour ago," Joe said. "Amanda was driving, and Doug was with her. They haven't come back."

"Did they go upriver or down?"

"I don't know. I only saw the boat in the creek. Once they'd passed the gas dock, they were out of sight."

"Is Frank there?"

"No. He and Aunt Myra have gone to Cincinnati."

"All right." The voice was brisk, but calm and controlled. "I'll call Bill Randolph and get him to come down to the marina. He can take his boat upriver and we'll head downriver. You can drive your uncle's boat, can't you?"

"I—I don't think so, sir," Joe admitted.

"All right then, I'll drive. I should be there in about five minutes, if I can reach Bill. I'll be there in any case. Did the forecast say where the storms are now?"

"No, just that they're advancing toward town."

"All right. If we hurry, we might be able to get out and find the Peg. If not . . ." He didn't finish. "Five minutes," he repeated, and hung up.

It was only a little more than five minutes, but it seemed hours before the dark blue car pulled into the marina parking lot. It was followed by another car. A man and a boy got out of the other car and joined James Sterling. "Joe Schmidt?" the mayor asked, reaching out to shake hands.

166

Joe nodded and took his hand. "This is Bill Randolph and his son Steve." They all exchanged nods, and James Sterling looked up at the sky. "What do you think?" he asked the others.

Bill Randolph shook his head. "I don't like the look of it. Or the feel of it, either."

"Come on, Dad," Steve said. "We have to go. If they're out there when the storm hits . . ."

"And what if we're out there when it hits? Suppose Amanda's had the good sense to get off the river. Then they'd be all right and we'd be in trouble."

James Sterling nodded. "He's right, Steve." A low, deep rumbling had begun. "Listen to that. There's no point risking four other people and two other boats. We don't even know where they went. And if they did tie up in a creek, we'd pass them without knowing it."

"But—" Steve didn't go on. There was nothing to say. Joe knew how he felt. He, too, wanted to go out, to do something. But the odds were against them.

Even as they stood there, the sky was darkening noticeably. Off to the southwest, lightning flashed. James Sterling shook his head. "We'll just have to wait it out and hope for the best. They could still get back, of course, just ahead of it. Amanda might try to outrun it if she's close. Otherwise, she'd have the sense to get tied up somewhere. "Can we wait at the coffee shop, Joe?"

"Sure." Joe led the way and unlocked the door. As they went inside and turned on the lights, the first heavy drops of rain were speckling the parking lot. A few minutes later, the storm hit with incredible force, battering the coffee shop windows with rain so heavy it looked as if buckets of water were being tossed at the building. Lightning flashed almost continuously and the thunder was deafening. Joe wondered what it would be like to be out in a boat in such a storm. It was frightening even in here. If the tornado siren should start, there was no place to go—no basement. No basement on a boat, either, he thought.

It was so dark outside that he could see the mercury vapor light in the parking lot begin to glow on. The four of them sat at the counter, not talking, just listening to the violence outside. Joe was about to offer to make coffee, hoping that would help somehow, when the lights flickered twice and went out.

In the blue-white flashes of lightning, Joe looked at the silhouettes of the others. They looked carved out of stone, a combination of impatience and fear that none of them wished to acknowledge. They paid no attention to the darkness, just sat and waited.

At last, the wind began to die down and the lightning flashed less frequently. An occasional thunderclap still crashed above the building, but the storm was passing. It was still raining heavily when James Sterling stood up. "Okay. By the time we can get the boats out, it ought to be safe enough. Let's go."

The others leaped to their feet. Outside, the rain drenched them quickly. The parking lot was running with water, heavy brown streams gathering and cutting into the grass along the drive to the boat ramp. The sky was lighter now, and Joe could see that the marina had not escaped damage. A cabin cruiser's canvas had been nearly torn away and was draped over its side into the water. An inflatable life raft had blown off the top of a houseboat and was lying upside down and limp over one of the concrete stanchions that anchored the docks.

"You go upriver," James Sterling said to the Randolphs, "and we'll go down. Don't bother with the creeks yet. If they were off the river, they're probably okay. Check both

banks. How long did you say they'd been gone?" he asked
Joe.

"About an hour before I called you."

"If they were cruising all that time, they could be pretty
far."

Joe reminded him that the river conditions weren't good
for speed.

"True. If they went upriver, the current would slow
them more. But if they were going with the current—we'll
just have to see."

"It'll be getting dark soon," Steve said.

"Does your spotlight work?"

Bill Randolph nodded. "We could go on looking after
dark if we just had to watch the banks. But if there's too
much junk in the water . . ."

James Sterling nodded. "Just go as far as you can while
the light lasts. If we all get back without finding them,
we'll call the sheriff's office and get some help."

James Sterling handled the Marina Queen as if he were
used to fifty-foot houseboats, Joe thought. He probably was.
For the first time in his life, Joe felt incompetent. In this
situation, he was barely more than excess baggage. He was
still so new to the river that he couldn't get out of his mind
the craziness of going out to rescue Amanda in the boat he
lived on, his bedroom tagging behind, his dirty dishes in
the sink, the legal pad half-filled with his story still on the
table.

"Would you go out on the front deck when we get to the
river?" James Sterling said. He was standing at the wheel,
peering ahead into the rain. The single windshield wiper
slashed back and forth in front of him. "I'd like you to keep
an eye out for logs and whatever else might be out there.
Does Frank carry a battery spotlight?"

"I think so." He opened the emergency-equipment locker and found it.

"Take it out with you. We can use all the help we can get."

Joe took the spotlight and went out to the rail on the front deck. A wave broke over the bow, and he was about to back away, when he realized it made no difference. He was already soaked to the skin. The rain was still coming down, but not as hard.

Joe switched on the light and moved it back and forth across the water in front of them. It was light enough now that he didn't really need it, but it gave him a sense of doing something concrete. He thought about Stephen Randolph and his father, doing this same thing. He hoped that if Amanda was out here, in trouble, it would be the Marina Queen that would find her. He knew nothing about Steve Randolph, of course, except what Doug had told him, that he was—or had been—Amanda's boyfriend. But it took only one look to know that Steve and Amanda had a lot in common. Out here on the river was a whole life the two of them had shared, a life Joe Schmidt knew nothing about. At least, he thought, let me find her. At least let there be that between us.

The storm had done its damage along the river, too. Trees, whose roots had been exposed by the flood, had toppled, their still green branches dragging in the water with the current. If the Peg had been tied up along the bank, Joe hoped it hadn't been tied to one of those. Some of them looked as if they could crush a cabin cruiser to kindling.

He shivered. The rain had stopped now, but the air against his wet clothes was freezing. The spotlight picked out the edges of the logs and branches they kept passing. So far, James Sterling had seen them nearly as soon as he

170

had, and had avoided them. They were traveling down the middle of the river, watching both banks. But aside from the fallen trees and the rusting hulk of an old barge, they had seen nothing.

After nearly an hour, when dusk was beginning to close down on them, Joe saw what looked like a cruiser, heeled over against the bank on the Ohio side, in a stretch of dense, low willows. He couldn't tell for sure whether it was the Peg or not. He aimed the spotlight at it, but the beam didn't reach that far. Just as he was about to point it out to James Sterling, the boat angled toward it. "Do you think that's her?" Joe called.

"I wish I didn't," was the answer.

But as they came closer, the outline of the cruiser became clear. It was the Peg. Joe could see no movement around it. Had it been thrown against the bank during the storm, or had it been tied there, and merely pushed over? He hoped it had been tied.

James Sterling nosed the houseboat into the bank downriver from the Peg, in a stretch clear of undergrowth. "Grab the starboard springline and get us tied to a tree upstream," he called as the bow thudded heavily against the mud.

"What?"

"The rope halfway back on the right!" he said. "Fast!"

Joe hurried along the side of the cabin and found the rope coiled on the rail. He took it and went forward, stepping out of his thongs and jumping barefoot into the water. James Sterling stayed at the wheel, keeping the engines idling until Joe had the line around the tree. Then he was out of the boat and running, slipping in the mud, toward the Peg.

Amanda had no idea how much time had passed. She sat, shivering, next to Doug, who had not moved, and scarcely seemed to be breathing. She'd lost count of the number of times she'd repeated "please," begging she didn't know who or what to keep Doug alive. She didn't know how bad the wound on his head was, but she had never seen anything as frightening as a person unconscious, unwakable. It was as if all the "Doug" had gone out of him. Everything that made him who he was, seemed to be gone, leaving just this smooth, cool figure no more like Doug than a statue would be.

She had just begun to notice the gradual darkening of the sky again—this time, with the coming of night—when she heard the sound of a boat engine. It was already close. She wanted to rush out, to shout and wave and be sure they saw her, but she couldn't seem to move, and she didn't want to leave Doug. Anyway, the boat was coming closer. Whoever it was had seen them.

The engine stopped then, and soon after a figure filled the companionway of the tilted cabin. A flashlight blinded her momentarily, then moved to Doug. "Is he—okay?"

It was her father. Amanda shook her head. "I don't know. He's unconscious." And then she burst into tears. The dark, familiar figure of her father splashed awkwardly toward her. She stood up, stiffly, and almost fell. His arms were around her then, tight, reassuring. Pain lanced through her arm, but she did her best to ignore it. She wasn't alone with her terror anymore.

He let her go. "Are you all right?"

"It's just my wrist. I think I broke it."

"Can you get out of the boat?"

"Yes," she said, rubbing the tears out of her eyes.

"Then go out and tell Joe to get in here. I'll need help getting Doug out."

Joe? Joe was here? Amanda's heart leaped. But she hadn't wanted to see Joe again. She moved carefully around her father, who had bent over Doug and was playing his light over the wound on his head.

She slipped several times trying to get up the slanted stairs. When she got herself over the Peg's side and onto the riverbank, Joe was there and caught her as she nearly fell again. Her arm was a mass of throbbing pain. "Dad wants you to help him. Doug's hurt—unconscious."

Joe held her for a moment, searching her face. "Are you okay?"

"Yes. Go get Doug."

They carried Doug between them, moving slowly, slipping and catching themselves, until they'd maneuvered him up from the cabin and out onto the bank. Amanda watched helplessly, wishing there was something she could do. James Sterling took Doug then, while Joe put down the houseboat's gangplank. They laid Doug on the couch in the front cabin, with a towel under his head, and covered him with a blanket. Amanda could barely see Joe as he coiled the springline and put it back, then stowed the gangplank.

"We'll come for the Peg tomorrow," her father said as he backed the Marina Queen away from the shore. "She isn't going anywhere."

Amanda, huddled under a blanket in the armchair next to the couch, felt tears spilling down her cheeks again. The Peg was wrecked, and she had done it. And Doug—she didn't want to think about what had happened to him. Her father clicked on the running lights, called to Joe to use the spotlight again, and headed the Queen slowly against the current. When he'd adjusted her speed, he radioed for an ambulance to meet them at the marina. "We can't waste any time getting him to the hospital," he said, when he'd finished his transmission. After that, he didn't speak again, just watched the water ahead, occasionally steering in accord with Joe's shouted directions. Amanda wished he would yell, tell her how wrong it had been to take the boat out, how stupid to forget the weather radio. Then, maybe she could even yell back. But except for a glance at Doug now and then, he did nothing but concentrate on driving the boat.

The rest of the way to the marina, Amanda felt herself drifting. She couldn't tell whether she was awake or dreaming. Thoughts and images were jumbled, a crazy mixture of feelings, colors, sounds. *I'm sorry*, she'd think, and the words would echo as if bouncing off the walls of a cave. But before the echoes could die away would come the denial. *No. Not sorry. It wasn't my fault*. It was her father's fault. He had driven her away from the house. He was the one who had caused this disintegration of everything. Images of earthquakes, of buildings falling with the sound of thunder. The world collapsing and dust rising over the rubble. His fault! *I'm sorry, I'm sorry, I'm sorry!*

Then there was a confusion of people and lights and voices. She was lifted by strong hands, put on a stretcher, a blanket drawn tightly around her. "No," she said. "Not me. It's Doug. I'm okay. It's Doug!" But the voices hushed her. She felt herself bumping up and then down again. Doors were closed. In the darkness, she heard a siren start. She had never ridden in an ambulance. To her right, she could see a white shape across an open space. Doug. *Please*, she thought again.

Her father was there too, she saw. Between them. She felt a hand on her shoulder and closed her eyes, as if to shut out Doug's stillness, the pain in her arm, and most of all, the weight of her father's hand.

·14·

Amanda opened her eyes and found herself looking at a square light set into a white ceiling. She started to sit up, then lay back. Her left arm felt heavy, and she saw that it was encased in a white cast. She remembered something about that, voices and pain and a needle, she thought, but it was hard to sort out. The memories seemed to come in little pieces, like disconnected film shorts. There had been a bright, harsh light in her eyes, a white curtain that moved with a swishing, clinking sound, and faces she didn't recognize. All the time, she had wanted to ask someone about Doug, but they only wanted to fuss over her. She looked down toward the end of the bed and saw that her father was there, standing just inside the doorway, watching her. "How do you feel?" he asked.

She thought about the question for a moment. It was hard to tell, really. There was a pain somewhere, she knew, but it didn't seem to have anything to do with her. "How's Doug?"

Her father smiled, and the gray weariness of his face seemed to lift for a moment. "He's going to be fine. He won't be up and around by tomorrow—he had a bad concussion and it took fourteen stitches to close him up—but he's awake."

Amanda thanked whoever or whatever she'd been begging, that long cold time in the boat. Doug was all right, or would be all right, so the hard knot of fear would go away. Her father was standing as if he couldn't decide whether to stay there or not. She had never seen him looking the way he did now. His shirt was stained with blood, his muddy trousers torn, his face dirty. "Tarnished," she thought, and closed her eyes.

"Your mother's on her way back from Michigan," he said.

"Did you tell her about the Peg?"

"She says, and I quote, 'It's only a boat.'"

Not worthy of love, Amanda thought. But then, who is? "Can I see Doug?"

"You can later, after you've had a little rest."

"But I'm not hurt," Amanda said. "Except for this." She raised the cast, and the pain that seemed to be loose in the room increased.

"Abrasions and contusions," her father said. "You're about to discover what that expression means. When the painkiller they gave you wears off, you won't be so eager to get up. A day or two in bed is what you need."

"Is that what I need?" she asked. She wished she could believe it. She wished that a broken bone and some bruises were all that was wrong with her.

Her father moved up beside the bed and put a hand against her cheek. She turned away and looked at the window, where the bed, her father, and the door into the hall were reflected against the darkness outside. She concentrated on looking through the reflection, focusing her eyes on a light in the hospital parking lot. "I guess I'm supposed to apologize," she said after a while.

"What do you think?"

"I don't know."

"There are things that can't be fixed by saying I'm sorry."

"Then how can they be fixed?" Amanda thought, and realized she had said it out loud.

Her father didn't answer. She turned back to look at him. His hand was still on the pillow next to her head, but he didn't touch her again. "Sometimes they can't," he said finally. A cart rumbled by in the hall outside, full of clinking glasses. "But you can't really know that until you try. It depends on whether you believe it's worth trying, I suppose."

Amanda closed her eyes again. She wasn't sure she was up to trying. What she wanted was a time machine that would take her back before things had gone wrong, before there was anything to fix.

"You have some visitors," her father said. "Steve and his father went out looking for you, too."

"Steve's here?" She hadn't seen him since he'd let her out of the car to walk home. She couldn't very well shut a door now and refuse to talk to him, not after he'd gone out on the river to find her. What difference did it make now, anyway? He'd been right about her father anyway—just like everybody else.

"Joe's here too."

How could she have Joe and Steve here together? What was the alternative? She sighed. If they didn't come in together, she'd have to choose who she'd see first. She knew who that would be, but it was a bigger task than she could handle now to explain it to anyone. "Tell them to come in."

"But just for a minute," her father said. "You need to sleep."

And then they came in and stood on each side of her

bed. She looked from one to the other and tilted her mouth in what she hoped looked like a proper smile. "Hi. I guess I should thank you both."

Steve smiled his big, white-toothed smile. "It's Joe you should thank. If he hadn't seen you leave the marina, no one would have known you were out there."

Joe looked as bad as her father. His jeans and T-shirt were muddy, his face was dirty, his hair hung limply over his forehead in little clumps. She wondered if he could still be wet. How long had it been? Steve, on the other hand, looked about the way he always did. His hair was freshly combed, his rugby shirt—with the alligator—and cut-offs were clean. He hadn't found the Peg, though, hadn't had to scramble through the mud. It wasn't his fault.

"I should have tried to stop you," Joe said.

"I shouldn't have gone," Amanda admitted. She knew it had been the unspoken thought behind Steve's words, beneath his smile.

"Anyway," Steve said, "all's well that ends well."

"Sure," Amanda said. She caught the look Joe had given Steve, and suspected Joe knew things had not ended at all. Certainly, not well.

James Sterling clapped a hand on Steve's shoulder. "Time to go. You can come back tomorrow, Steve."

Amanda looked at Joe and he shrugged. "You, too," she said. Joe's face was bland, unsmiling, but his eyes seemed to be grinning at her. As her father ushered the boys out into the hall, Joe waved. Amanda waved back.

"Sleep now," her father said, as he closed the door.

She had a great deal to think about, but her mind wouldn't stay focused. The images began to swirl around her again and she let them come, unwilling to try to make sense of them. The pain was still there, a presence in the room, and she wondered how she could know it was there, feel it, really, without hurting. And then she was asleep.

Amanda's lunch tray had just been taken away the next day when Joe came in. Sun was streaming through the window, and even with only a sheet over her, Amanda was hot. Her body ached everywhere, and it seemed impossible to move without making something worse. But Joe looked great. His hair was combed, he was wearing clean jeans and a short-sleeved plaid shirt. The look he gave her seemed to go straight through her. This time, she didn't need to make an effort to smile.

"Enough of this goldbricking!" he said. "You have work to do."

"Goldbricking?" Amanda started to sit up, and fell back, grimacing from the pain. "Have you ever had abrasions and contusions?"

"Not in quantity," he admitted.

"Then don't belittle them. They hurt!"

"I believe you. But you still have work to do. They say you're going home first thing tomorrow, so you've got to be a big sister while you're here. They just told Doug he isn't allowed to read! They won't let him sit up, or even raise his head because of the concussion—they have to feed him. He was coping with that all right, but when he asked for a book and they told him the bad news, he had a fit. He needs somebody to read to him."

"I ought to be able to handle that."

"Of course. We'll pop you into a wheelchair and take you down to his room. From what I've seen around here, we can't ask the nurses to read to him—they wouldn't be able to handle the vocabulary of any of his books. I can't

179

take you down till later, though, because he's supposed to take a nap. I don't think hospital life agrees with Doug."

"Does it agree with anybody?"

Joe sat in the chair next to the bed. "I would have brought you flowers, but I hate them."

"You hate flowers?"

"Not in general. I hate them in hospitals. I was laid up for three weeks once, after a motorcycle accident—my brother had kindly taken me for a ride—and I had flowers. I had to lie there and watch those flowers die one by one. The nurses used to come in every day and take the dead ones out, so the bouquets got scrawnier and scrawnier, till there was nothing left but those green things. I think they wax those or something. It was awful! So I'd never take anybody flowers."

"I never thought of it that way."

"Actually, I didn't bring you anything. Sorry."

Amanda pushed the hair back off her face. "Listen, it's enough that you came. How'd you get off work?"

"Funny thing about that. I have an unusually under-standing boss." He laughed. "You should have heard Uncle Frank on the subject of that storm. All the way to Cincinnati and the game was rained out! And besides that, he missed the action at home. You should be glad he wasn't around last night, though. He was pretty upset at you for taking the boat out."

"It was dumb."

"Which isn't like you, Uncle Frank said. Why *did* you?" Amanda stared at the plaster cast sticking out from the wide sleeve of the blue-dotted hospital gown and didn't answer. "Has your father been in to see you today?" She shook her head. "I didn't think so. He seems to think you'd rather not have him here."

180

"He's right." Amanda felt her eyes filling with tears and turned her head away.

Joe picked up a blue plastic pitcher from the tray table next to the bed. "It's hot in here. You mind if I have a drink?" She shook her head, and he poured ice water into a glass. He remembered how certain she had been that her father was innocent, how absolute her faith in him had been. It wasn't hard to figure out why she'd taken the boat out. Whatever had happened between them, it had left her father to hover around Doug, joke with him, and then pace the halls, unwilling or unable to come into Amanda's room. "Are you making yourself an orphan, too?"

She looked back at him and the tears spilled over. She hated to cry, particularly when somebody could see her. "Just for a handful of silver, he left us," she said.

"He didn't leave."

"He might as well have left. It's as if he's a different person now."

"Maybe you just didn't know, before, who he was."

"It ends up the same."

Joe drained the glass of water. "I seem to remember a conversation yesterday afternoon about knowing people."

Amanda remembered it. And she remembered what Joe had said about love. But now it didn't seem to make as much sense as it had then. Did love count if the person you thought you loved didn't really exist? "A handful of silver," she said. It kept coming back to that.

"If you're going to remember quotations, I have a better one for you. From a better poet, anyway."

"What is it?"

"It's Thel's Motto. From William Blake's *Book of Thel.*" He cleared his throat. "You have to listen carefully, now. This is Blake. 'Does the Eagle know what is in the

181

pit? Or wilt thou go ask the Mole? Can Wisdom be put in a silver rod? Or Love in a golden bowl?' "

Amanda frowned "I don't understand it."

"I was with your father last night, Amanda, when he had to wait out that storm, not knowing where you were or what might be happening to you."

"And?"

"And he was hurting. Then, and while we were looking for you, and after we'd found you. He was hurting."

"So was I."

"Do you think he doesn't know that?"

Amanda remembered what her father had said about apologies. "Would you pour me some of that water?" she asked.

Joe poured the water and put a straw in the glass. "Here." As he watched her drink, he remembered James Sterling's face lit by lightning, the fear and pain mixed, he knew, with anger. "Watching your father last night made me think about my own father. And about myself. Nothing's ever as simple as people tell you it is. Feelings get all mixed together, sometimes. I got to wondering if I was the only one at home who was being hurt. I've been so concerned about myself and how my father doesn't understand me, that I've never even tried to know how he must feel to have a son like me. Just because people don't always show their feelings, it doesn't mean they don't have them. My father and I may not understand each other, but I'm not so sure anymore that it's anybody's fault."

"So what are you going to do?"

"For starters, I'll go home and talk to him. It might not change anything, but it can't hurt."

"What about school?"

"Maybe working for a while won't be all bad. Uncle Frank says he could keep me busy all year if I want to stay a while. And meantime, there's no reason why I can't go on writing. School will be there when I get there. And maybe Dad will even change his mind. Who knows?"

"No more orphan?"

"No more orphan." She handed the glass to him, and their fingers touched as he took it. "Not by choice!"

"Could you give me that quotation again? What is it?"

"Thel's Motto. 'Does the Eagle know what is in the pit? Or wilt thou go ask the Mole? Can Wisdom be put in a silver rod? Or Love in a golden bowl?' "

"Do you understand it?"

"What it means to me may not be what it meant to Blake, but that's poetry. For me it's a little like that saying about walking a mile in the other guy's moccasins. If you live in the sky, you can't know what it's like to live underground. We don't know what it is to be somebody else. There's more to it than that, of course."

"What if you can't tell the eagles from the moles?"

"Maybe you don't have to." He took her hand. "He says you can't measure wisdom. Or love."

Amanda closed her eyes and for a moment, she was back in the Peg—cold, terrified, alone. As she'd waited, she'd gone over and over all the things she had done wrong. From deciding to go out in the first place, she'd broken nearly every rule there was; she'd been stupid and thoughtless and criminally careless, and she didn't know if Doug, so still beside her, would even survive. Then her father had been there, and it was enough to have his arms around her, to know she was safe. She opened her eyes and squeezed Joe's hand. That touch, too, was enough. "I think you may be right. Blake may be better than Browning. But I have to think about it a little."

"It can't hurt." He stood up and sat next to her on the edge of the bed, smoothing her hair. She touched his cheek, and he took her in his arms, kissing her gently, but lingeringly.

When he pulled away, she smiled up at him. This kiss had been more than a handshake, she knew. "The contusions aren't as bad as I thought they were."

"It's all in the mind," he said. "I'm going to go see when Doug will be ready for his reader."

"You're not leaving?"

"I'll be back." He kissed her on the nose. "I'm milady's chauffeur, remember? I'm going to push the chair!"

"All right. But don't be long."

"I won't be. I promise." He went to the door, looked out into the hall, and turned back to Amanda. "There's a man pacing around out here—"

"Anybody I know?"

"There's a certain family resemblance."

Amanda took a deep breath and then smiled. "If he looks like he might be my father, you'd better tell him to come in."

F
TOL   Tolan, Stephanie S.

           No safe harbors